ANNIE HAYNES
THE HOUSE IN CHARLTON CRESCENT

Annie Haynes was born in 1865, the daughter of an ironmonger.

By the first decade of the twentieth century she lived in London and moved in literary and early feminist circles. Her first crime novel, *The Bungalow Mystery*, appeared in 1923, and another nine mysteries were published before her untimely death in 1929.

Who Killed Charmian Karslake? appeared posthumously, and a further partially-finished work, *The Crystal Beads Murder*, was completed with the assistance of an unknown fellow writer, and published in 1930.

Also by Annie Haynes

The Bungalow Mystery
The Abbey Court Murder
The Secret of Greylands
The Blue Diamond
The Witness on the Roof
The Crow's Inn Tragedy
The Master of the Priory
The Man with the Dark Beard
The Crime at Tattenham Corner
Who Killed Charmian Karslake?
The Crystal Beads Murder

ANNIE HAYNES

THE HOUSE IN CHARLTON CRESCENT

With an introduction
by Curtis Evans

DEAN STREET PRESS

Published by Dean Street Press 2015

All Rights Reserved

First published in 1926 by The Bodley Head

Cover by DSP
Cover illustration shows detail from 'Autumn
Midnight' (1923) by Eric Gill

Introduction © Curtis Evans 2015

ISBN 978 1 911095 03 3

www.deanstreetpress.co.uk

THE MYSTERY OF THE MISSING AUTHOR

Annie Haynes and Her Golden Age
Detective Fiction

THE PSYCHOLOGICAL ENIGMA of Agatha Christie's notorious 1926 vanishing has continued to intrigue Golden Age mystery fans to the present day. The Queen of Crime's eleven-day disappearing act is nothing, however, compared to the decades-long disappearance, in terms of public awareness, of between-the-wars mystery writer Annie Haynes (1865-1929), author of a series of detective novels published between 1923 and 1930 by Agatha Christie's original English publisher, The Bodley Head. Haynes's books went out of print in the early Thirties, not long after her death in 1929, and her reputation among classic detective fiction readers, high in her lifetime, did not so much decline as dematerialize. When, in 2013, I first wrote a piece about Annie Haynes' work, I knew of only two other living persons besides myself who had read any of her books. Happily, Dean Street Press once again has come to the rescue of classic mystery fans seeking genre gems from the Golden Age, and is republishing all Haynes' mystery novels. Now that her crime fiction is coming back into print, the question naturally arises: Who Was Annie Haynes? Solving the mystery of this forgotten author's lost life has taken leg work by literary sleuths on two continents (my thanks for their assistance to Carl Woodings and Peter Harris).

Until recent research uncovered new information about Annie Haynes, almost nothing about her was publicly known besides the fact of her authorship of twelve mysteries during the Golden Age of detective fiction. Now we know that she led an altogether intriguing life, too soon cut short by disability and death, which took her from the isolation of the rural English Midlands in the nineteenth century to the cultural high life of Edwardian London. Haynes was born in 1865 in the Leicestershire town of Ashby-de-la-Zouch, the first child of ironmonger Edwin Haynes and Jane (Henderson) Haynes, daughter of Montgomery Henderson, longtime superintendent of the gardens at nearby Coleorton Hall, seat of the Beaumont baronets. After her father left his family, young Annie resided with her grandparents at the gardener's cottage at Coleorton Hall, along with her mother and younger brother. Here Annie doubtlessly obtained an acquaintance with the ways of the country gentry that would serve her well in her career as a genre fiction writer.

We currently know nothing else of Annie Haynes' life in Leicestershire, where she still resided (with her mother) in 1901, but by 1908, when Haynes was in her early forties, she was living in London with Ada Heather-Bigg (1855-1944) at the Heather-Bigg family home, located halfway between Paddington Station and Hyde Park at 14 Radnor Place, London. One of three daughters of Henry Heather-Bigg, a noted pioneer in the development of orthopedics and artificial limbs, Ada Heather-Bigg was a prominent Victorian and Edwardian era feminist and social reformer. In the 1911 British census entry for 14 Radnor Place, Heather-Bigg, a "philanthropist and journalist," is listed as the head of the household and Annie Haynes, a "novelist," as a "visitor," but in fact Haynes would remain there with Ada Heather-Bigg until Haynes' death in 1929.

Haynes' relationship with Ada Heather-Bigg introduced the aspiring author to important social sets in England's great metropolis. Though not a novelist herself, Heather-Bigg was an important figure in the city's intellectual milieu, a well-connected feminist activist of great energy and passion who believed strongly in the idea of women attaining economic independence through remunerative employment. With Ada Heather-Bigg behind her, Annie Haynes's writing career had powerful backing indeed. Although in the 1911 census Heather-Bigg listed Haynes' occupation as "novelist," it appears that Haynes did not publish any novels in book form prior to 1923, the year that saw the appearance of *The Bungalow Mystery*, which Haynes dedicated to Heather-Bigg. However, Haynes was a prolific producer of newspaper serial novels during the second decade of the twentieth century, penning such works as *Lady Carew's Secret, Footprints of Fate, A Pawn of Chance, The Manor Tragedy* and many others.

Haynes' twelve Golden Age mystery novels, which appeared in a tremendous burst of creative endeavor between 1923 and 1930, like the author's serial novels retain, in stripped-down form, the emotionally heady air of the nineteenth-century triple-decker sensation novel, with genteel settings, shocking secrets, stormy passions and eternal love all at the fore, yet they also have the fleetness of Jazz Age detective fiction. Both in their social milieu and narrative pace Annie Haynes' detective novels bear considerable resemblance to contemporary works by Agatha Christie; and it is interesting to note in this regard that Annie Haynes and Agatha Christie were the only female mystery writers published by The Bodley Head, one of the more notable English mystery imprints in the early Golden Age. "A very remarkable feature of recent detective fiction," observed the *Illustrated London News* in 1923, "is the skill displayed by women in this branch of story-telling. Isabel Ostrander, Carolyn Wells, Annie Haynes and last, but very far from least, Agatha Christie, are contesting the laurels of Sherlock Holmes' creator with a great spirit, ingenuity and success." Since Ostrander and Wells were American authors, this left Annie Haynes, in the estimation of the *Illustrated London News*, as the main British female competitor to Agatha Christie. (Dorothy L. Sayers, who, like Haynes, published her debut mystery novel in 1923, goes unmentioned.) Similarly, in 1925 *The Sketch* wryly noted that "[t]ired men, trotting home at the end of an imperfect day, have been known to pop into the library and ask for an Annie Haynes. They have not made a mistake in the street number. It is not a cocktail they are asking for...."

Twenties critical opinion adjudged that Annie Haynes' criminous concoctions held appeal not only for puzzle fiends impressed with the "considerable craftsmanship" of their plots (quoting from the *Sunday Times* review of *The Bungalow Mystery*), but also for more general readers attracted to their purely literary qualities. "Not only a crime story of merit, but also a novel which will interest readers to whom mystery for its own sake has little appeal," avowed *The Nation* of Haynes' *The Secret of Greylands*, while the *New Statesman* declared of *The Witness on the Roof* that "Miss Haynes has a sense of character; her people are vivid and not the usual puppets of detective fiction." Similarly, the *Bookman* deemed the characters in Haynes' *The Abbey Court Murder* "much truer to life than is the case in many sensational stories" and *The Spectator* concluded of *The Crime at Tattenham Corner*, "Excellent as a detective tale, the book also is a charming novel."

Sadly, Haynes' triumph as a detective novelist proved short lived. Around 1914, about the time of the outbreak of the Great War, Haynes had been stricken with debilitating rheumatoid arthritis that left her in constant pain and hastened her death from heart failure in 1929, when she was only 63. Haynes wrote several of her detective novels on fine days in Kensington Gardens, where she was wheeled from 14 Radnor Place in a bath chair, but in her last years she was able only to travel from her bedroom to her study. All of this was an especially hard blow for a woman who had once been intensely energetic and quite physically active.

In a foreword to *The Crystal Beads Murder*, the second of Haynes' two posthumously published mysteries, Ada Heather-Bigg noted that Haynes' difficult daily physical struggle "was materially lightened by the warmth of friendships" with other authors and by the "sympathetic and friendly relations between her and her publishers." In this latter instance Haynes' experience rather differed from that of her sister Bodleian, Agatha Christie, who left The Bodley Head on account of what she deemed an iniquitous contract that took unjust advantage of a naive young author. Christie moved, along with her landmark detective novel *The Murder of Roger Ackroyd* (1926), to Collins and never looked back, enjoying ever greater success with the passing years.

At the time Christie crossed over to Collins, Annie Haynes had only a few years of life left. After she died at 14 Radnor Place on 30 March 1929, it was reported in the press that "many people well-known in the literary world" attended the author's funeral at St. Michaels and All Angels Church, Paddington, where her sermon was delivered by the eloquent vicar, Paul Nichols, brother of the writer Beverley Nichols and dedicatee of Haynes' mystery novel *The Master of the Priory*; yet by the time of her companion Ada Heather-Bigg's death in 1944, Haynes and her once highly-praised mysteries were forgotten. (Contrastingly, Ada Heather-Bigg's name survives today in the University College of London's Ada Heather-Bigg Prize in Economics.) Only three of Haynes' novels were ever published in the United States, and she passed away less than a year before the formation of the Detection Club, missing any chance of being invited to join this august body of distinguished British detective novelists. Fortunately, we have today entered, when it comes to classic mystery, a period of rediscovery and revival, giving a reading audience a chance once again, after over eighty years, to savor the detective fiction fare of Annie Haynes. *Bon appétit!*

Curtis Evans

CHAPTER I

LADY ANNE DAVENTRY was not a pleasant old lady. Her nearest and dearest found her difficult to get on with, her servants called her "cantankerous," and her contemporaries—those who remembered her in her far-off beautiful youth—said she had a good heart.

She was not so very old really, not as people count age nowadays. More than a whole year lay between her and that seventieth birthday that makes such a very definite landmark in most people's lives. Trouble and ill-health had combined to make her look far older than her actual years. No one would have thought her younger than her only remaining brother—The Rev. and Hon. Augustus Fyvert—the rector of North Coton. Yet, in reality, Lady Anne had been a child in the nursery when he was a big boy going to Eton.

Life had not been kind to Lady Anne. The parents, whose petted darling she had been, had both died without seeing their youngest and most dearly-loved child grow up, and the man to whom she had been engaged in her youth, and whom she had passionately loved, had been false to her. Her subsequent marriage with Squire Daventry, of Daventry Keep, had been in the nature of a compromise, and her life with him had not been an easy one. One consolation she had had—the two bonny boys, who grew up to handsome manhood within the walls of Daventry Keep. Then, following swiftly on the old Squire's death, had come the great war; Christopher Daventry and his brother Frank had both died gloriously, fighting for England and freedom, and Lady Anne was left desolate.

The effect upon her of the double blow was devastating. For a time they feared for Lady Anne's life and reason, but she was not made of the stuff that goes under. Her vigorous vitality reasserted itself, and very soon Lady Anne came out into the world once more.

But she was never quite the same; grief seemed to have hardened, not softened, her whole nature. She who had been gracious and charming became snappy and irritable, and finally, when the rheumatism, from which she had suffered for years, became chronic and brought about a permanent stiffness of the limbs, Lady Anne, while saying little of her sufferings, was a distinctly cross and unpleasant old lady.

In her boys' time she had lived principally at Daventry Keep, which, by the terms of the old Squire's will, remained hers for life, but after the death of her sons she had found the quiet of the country oppressive, and for years now she had rented on a long lease the town house of the Daventrys in Charlton Crescent.

It overlooked the Park, and from her bedroom windows she could watch the stream of London traffic ebbing and flowing along the capital's great artery.

Lady Anne's sitting-room was on the first floor and looked out on the beautiful old-world garden beyond. It remained unchanged in its Victorian splendour as it had been at the time of her marriage; there were no modern furnishing vagaries for Lady Anne. The floor was carpeted all over in luxurious velvet-pile—Lady Anne liked its warmth and softness—the curtains were of lovely old brocade in faded pinks and blues, that was matched in the comfortable, spacious arm-chairs and settees. There were panels of beautiful old tapestry on the walls, quaint old lustre and cut-glass ornaments on the high marble mantelpiece; daguerreotypes and old- fashioned photographs of the relatives and friends of Lady Anne's young days were everywhere. One table was devoted entirely to miniatures on ivory. There was even a spinet, which Lady Anne loved for the sake of the dear dead-and-gone women whose fingers had touched it, and a big jar of potpourri stood by one of the windows.

Lady Anne's escritoire was facing it—a very beautiful specimen of old Georgian workmanship. When let down for writing it disclosed a front and sides richly inlaid. The tiny drawers at each side had golden knobs. The cupboard in the middle, misnamed secret, had a door inlaid all over in a curious arabesque pattern, inset with ivory and jade, and in it gold, silver and copper were oddly mingled.

The big revolving chair before this table was Lady Anne's favourite seat. She came of a generation that did not believe in soft seats for themselves, even when crippled by rheumatism.

She was sitting there this morning, a quantity of papers on the slip-table before her, which she was perusing steadily and then docketing methodically on a small file. On her right hand there lay an open manuscript book, richly bound in grey and gold, with the word "Diary" scrawled across it in golden letters. She made several entries in this book as she filed her papers.

Every now and then her eyes strayed mechanically to the trees outside. It was evident that, busy as she seemed, her attention was wandering, her thoughts far away.

She was a picturesque figure in her black silk gown with its fichu of priceless old lace, a magnificent diamond crescent brooch gleaming amidst the filmy folds. Her still abundant snow-white hair was drawn back from her forehead over a Pompadour frame, and, with a fine disregard for the present fashion, coiled high on the top of her head and crowned with a tiny scrap of lace which she referred to sometimes as "my cap."

For the rest she was very pale; her skin with its network of wrinkles was the colour of old ivory. The once beautiful mouth had fallen in, but the big, very light blue eyes, beneath her still dark, straight brows, gave character to her face. Not on the whole an agreeable character! Lady Anne was an irritable, impatient old lady, and looked it!

At last she pushed the papers from her with a jerk, and opening one of the small drawers of the escritoire took out a tiny box, just a very ordinary-looking little pill-box. She opened it. Inside there were eight little pills, all sugar-coated; ordinary-looking enough contents for an ordinary box; yet Lady Anne's face went very white as she gazed at them.

Moving them very gingerly with the tip of her finger, she scrutinized each one with meticulous care as she did so.

"Yes, yes. There can be no doubt," she murmured to herself. Then, as if coming to some definite decision, she put on the lid of the pill-box firmly and laid it back in its place in the inlaid drawer. She waited again when she had pushed the drawer back.

Opposite, there hung a beautiful old mirror; Lady Anne loved that mirror. It had been given her when she was a young girl. She had taken it to the Keep when she married, and when she made up her mind to live in London she had brought the mirror with her. Now it seemed like an old friend. It had shown her herself as a young girl, as a bride, as a happy mother, then as a sorrow- stricken woman and one verging on old age, but never had there looked back at her such a reflection as she saw this morning. The cheeks, even the lips, were white. The big light eyes, still beautiful in shape and size, were wide with fear. Altogether the face in the glass looked like that of a woman oppressed by some terrible dread—some nameless horror!

Lady Anne stared straight at it for a minute or two as at the face of a stranger, then a long shiver shook her from head to foot. Like a woman returning from a trance she pressed her handkerchief over her lips, and turning back to her papers she drew from among them what looked like a list of business firms. She scrutinized it for a moment with knit brows, running her pen up and down the column as she did so; at last she stopped—Wilkins and Alleyn, Private Inquiry Agents, Parlere St., Strand, she read. "Yes, I think that is the firm."

She turned to the telephone which stood beside her and rang up Wilkins and Alleyn. Fortunately the line was clear and she was able to be put through at once. It was evidently a woman's voice that answered, and Lady Anne frowned. She had no opinion of her own sex in business.

"Messrs. Wilkins and Alleyn," she said sharply, "I wish to speak to one of the principals—Lady Anne Daventry."

There was a pause, and then a man's voice—a cultured man's voice—spoke:

"I am Bruce Cardyn, a junior partner in the firm of Messrs. Wilkins and Alleyn. You wished to speak to me?"

"Yes." Lady Anne's voice faltered, then gathered in strength as it went on. "I wish to consult a member of your firm. As I am a chronic invalid, unable to get out much, I cannot come to you. Besides, under the circumstances, I should not wish it to be known that I have paid a visit to your office, so I should be glad if one of your principals could call upon me as soon as possible. And I dare say that you will think this a strange request, but possibly you are used to them. Would you be kind enough to say at the door that you are applying for this post as secretary? I dismissed my secretary a few days ago and am now looking out for another. If you will allow it to be supposed that you are coming after the post, your being admitted will excite no surprise or suspicion in the household, and I am most anxious to avoid this."

Another pause. Lady Anne fancied that there was a consultation, then the same voice spoke again.

"Certainly. That would be the best plan. Would it suit you if I came in an hour's time?"

"Yes, it would," Lady Anne said decidedly. "Unless," she added grimly, "you could come in half an hour's time!"

Lady Anne did not move; very often on her bad days she did not go down to the dining-room for meals, but had something brought to her in her room. To-day, however, she gave orders that she was not to be disturbed until Mr. Cardyn's arrival.

It seemed a very long hour to her, and the soft spring gloaming had merged into something like darkness before Mr. Cardyn came.

The blinds had been closely drawn and the electric light turned on fully. In the old days Lady Anne had loved the twilight, but now she had got into the habit of glancing into the corners in a frightened fashion, and if she were alone the light was always turned on at the earliest possible moment.

She looked with curiosity at the man who came forward when the door closed.

"Mr. Bruce Cardyn?"

He bowed.

"You look very young," Lady Anne said discontentedly. "I hoped to see some one much older and with more experience."

Mr. Cardyn permitted himself a slight smile.

"I have had a good deal of experience and—I am not so young as I look, perhaps, Lady Anne; I am thirty-one."

"Are you indeed?" Lady Anne said incredulously, as she glanced at his fair, clean-shaven countenance, at the close-cut, fair hair, brushed straight back from his forehead, and the slim, youthful figure.

"I am, indeed," he confirmed.

"I heard of your firm from my friend, General Hetherington," Lady Anne resumed as she motioned him to a chair very close to her own. "I believe Messrs. Wilkins and Alleyn did some very successful work for him—not only discovered the criminal but recovered the stolen property. I am speaking of a burglary that took place at Hetherington Hall last year."

"I remember," Bruce Cardyn nodded. "Yes, we were fortunate enough to satisfy General Hetherington."

"But the General spoke of Messrs. Wilkins and Alleyn. I never heard him mention your name."

"I dare say not." Bruce Cardyn's smile deepened. "Yet I am the junior partner. My senior's name is Misterton. Wilkins and Alleyn is merely a—shall I say?—*nom de plume*. You see, if we visited you under our own names we should be more likely to be recognised by any professional crook who has read the list of private inquiry agents. If you will entrust your business to us, Lady Anne, I can promise that we will do our best for you."

"I believe you will. But it is no easy problem that I wish you to solve."

She stopped, and seemed for a moment to be really struggling for words in which to state her dilemma.

As Bruce Cardyn watched her the pity in his grey eyes grew and strengthened. There was something very pathetic about the stern old face, with the strong mouth that twitched every now and then, and the nameless dread looking out of the big shadowed eyes.

At last Lady Anne seemed to rally her courage by a supreme effort.

"Mr. Cardyn, I have never been a coward in my life—till now! And here to-day I am living in my own house, surrounded by servants, who have for the most part grown grey in my service, and by those who are bound to me by ties of blood and professed affection, yet—"

"Yet?" Bruce Cardyn echoed, a touch of surprise in his grey eyes.

Lady Anne looked at him, the faint colour that had come back to her withered cheeks ebbing once more; the dread in her eyes deepening. Her voice sank to a whisper:

"And yet, as I say, in my own house, surrounded by those I know and love, and who one would expect to have some sort of liking for me, some one is trying to kill me!"

It was not at all what Bruce Cardyn had expected to hear. He was silent for a minute. Sundry stories he had heard of old people who accused their own families of trying to murder them recurred to his mind, but Lady Anne was not old enough for that.

"You have some ground for your belief?" he hazarded at last.

Lady Anne bent her head.

"At first it was only a mere suspicion. I tried to smother it, to assure myself that it was only the merest fancy. I said to myself I am a disagreeable, snappy old woman, I know, but surely I am not so bad that anyone should wish to murder me. Now, however, conviction has been forced upon me. But, Mr. Cardyn, before we proceed, can you with as many underlings as you choose to bring, with any and every expense guaranteed, can you promise me safety in my own house?"

Bruce Cardyn's face was very grave. Lady Anne's aspect was so controlled, so direct, that the momentary suspicion that had flitted across his mind was dismissed finally and for ever.

"We will do our best to ensure your safety in every way, Lady Anne," he said steadily. "And I think we ought to succeed. More it is not in the power of mortal man to promise."

"It is not!" Lady Anne assented. "Well, Mr. Cardyn, I am going to trust you to safeguard me. Life is sweet to anyone, suppose, even when one is old and lonely. And we all shrink from the great abyss. Now, as I tell you, my life is being attempted, has been attempted by some member of my household, as I believe, and I want you to discover who it is, and to prevent the crime. But, above all things, I do not want the regular police called in. I want the whole thing kept as quiet as possible. I know that this will make your work more difficult, but I hope you will be none the less willing to undertake it."

"Certainly we will undertake it," Bruce Cardyn promised, his face pale and grave. "But first you can give some of the ground you have to go upon, Lady Anne?"

Lady Anne hesitated a minute, then she bent forward and took the pill-box again.

"I think this will show you best what I have to fear. Look!" She held the box toward him.

He put up a monocle and looked at its contents with great curiosity as it lay in his hand.

"The pills in that box originally were made up by the chemist I have employed for years, from a prescription given me by my own doctor. I was taking one the last thing every night. There were twelve in the box when it came. I took one at bed-time for five nights. I was glancing at them, only after I had taken the fifth; there were still eight left! What do you make of that?"

Mr. Cardyn looked at the pills; the gravity of his expression deepened.

"You are quite sure of your facts, Lady Anne. It would not be difficult, for instance, to make a mistake in the number of pills or of the number of nights you took them."

For answer, Lady Anne drew a small silver key from the handbag in front of her, and unlocked another small drawer. Inside was a sheet of embossed letter-paper. There were very few lines upon it, but the signature was one of the best known of the day:

DEAR LADY ANNE,

I have analysed the pills you sent me. Seven of them are harmless. The eighth contains hyoscine enough to kill ten women. I am returning them as you requested.

What can I do for you now? Please let me help you.

Yours always,

ROBERT SAINTSBURY.

"That," said Lady Anne very deliberately, "settles the question, I think!"

CHAPTER II

BRUCE CARDYN put the box down. "It certainly does appear to settle the question that some one is attempting your life. But—pardon me—it proves nothing with regard to the would-be assassin being a member of your household."

"Do you not think so?" Lady Anne questioned coldly. "Since the pills were kept in a drawer in my bedroom, it is difficult to see how anyone, not a member of my household, could have access to them."

"Difficult," Bruce Cardyn assented, "but not impossible. And, in a case of this kind, we cannot afford to rule out any possibilities, Lady Anne. But, now, is this all you have to go upon?"

"I am sorry to say it is not." Lady Anne's pale blue eyes were mechanically watching the flickering of the leaves on a branch of the creeper that had strayed over her window. "I have had several curious accidents, but the most serious of them all, to my mind, is this. To begin with, it is my custom to take a glass of hot milk the last thing at night. For some time I have not been feeling very well—indigestion, I thought it to be—and took my usual simple remedies without success.

"I am not over fond of doctors, but was beginning to think I should have to consult my old friend, Dr. Spencer, when, one night as I was drinking my milk, I became conscious of a very curious taste. It set me thinking. I put the glass down, meaning to make inquiries, and went on with my reading. Half an hour later, when the milk had got cold, my pet Persian cat, climbing about as she does sometimes, got on the table by my side and lapped up some of it before I noticed what she was doing. A very short time afterwards she was violently sick and lay writhing about in awful pain. I thought at first that she was going to die, but in the end got her round again. Since then I have taken no more hot milk. It goes down the drain, and I feel better. My indigestion is a thing of the past."

"And that is all?" Bruce Cardyn questioned.

"Is it not enough?" Lady Anne parried.

"It ought to be," Cardyn assented. "But, Lady Anne, have you no idea who is your would-be assassin?"

Lady Anne shook her head.

"None! Of course I do not say that my fancy has not strayed from one to another, and have said to myself—'it could not be so-and-so, it could not be so-and-so,' but of real knowledge, or even suspicion, I have none."

"I see."

There was a long pause. Cardyn sat with his eyes apparently studying the pattern of the carpet. At last he raised them and gave Lady Anne one long, penetrating look.

"Has anyone in the house any motive for desiring your death?"

"Every one of them," Lady Anne said slowly, a momentary moisture clouding her glasses. "Every servant in my employ comes in for a legacy at my death, small or large according to their time of service. This is well known and one which might have provided a motive."

"Exactly," Cardyn acquiesced. "And if the motive seems inadequate, one must remember for what exceedingly small sums murders have been committed in the past. Now will you tell me exactly of whom your household consists? First the servants?" He took out his note-book and waited.

Lady Anne's pale eyes gave him one swift look and then glanced obliquely away.

"To begin with there are Soames, the butler, and my maid, Pirnie. Both of them have been with me—with us—for many years. Pirnie came as quite a young girl, soon after my marriage. Then there are two housemaids, a kitchen-maid, and the cook-housekeeper, who has been here some years, a young footman under Soames, and a boy. That is all the indoor staff except that both the girls have maids—Miss Fyvert and Miss Balmaine, I mean. Outside we have a head gardener with a couple of men under him, and a chauffeur. But those, as I say, are out of count."

"I cannot at present put anyone out of count," Bruce Cardyn dissented, as he wrote a few lines rapidly in his note-book. "Now the members of your family, Lady Anne, please."

"They are soon told."

For a moment the detective fancied that Lady Anne's stern lips quivered; then he told himself that he must be mistaken as she went on in the same clear voice:

"There are my two nieces, Dorothy and Maureen Fyvert. They have made their home with me for the most part since their mother's death two years ago. Maureen is a child of twelve, usually at a boarding-school at Torquay, but at present at home on account of an outbreak of measles. Dorothy is twenty, and a very good girl. Then there is Margaret Balmaine, my husband's granddaughter."

She was not looking at the detective now or she would have seen his interested expression change to one of utter amazement.

"Miss Margaret Balmaine!" he repeated, but even as he spoke the veil of inscrutability dropped over his features once more, and he became again the impassive-looking detective.

"Has Miss Balmaine, too, been here for some time?"

"No, she is a comparatively recent comer," Lady Anne said quietly. "She has not been here quite three months as a matter of fact."

Cardyn was writing quickly now. "You said your husband's granddaughter?" he questioned.

"Yes," Lady Anne said, with another quick glance at the detective's sleek, bent head. "My husband had been married and lost his wife before he met me. He had one daughter who ran away and nearly broke her father's heart. She died many years ago in Australia, and we had no idea that she had left any children until this girl turned up a few months ago and introduced herself to me."

"She had, I presume, the necessary credentials?"

"Oh, yes. Quite so. Quite so!" Lady Anne assented. "My lawyer saw to that, naturally. And, as a matter of course, the girl is making her home with me while she remains in England.

Then, running up and down so often that, though he is not a member of my household, he might almost be reckoned as such, is John Daventry, my husband's nephew, who succeeded to the estate on the death of his—cousins."

There was a momentary break in the firm voice at the allusion to her dead sons, then she went on: "He is half engaged to my elder niece, Dorothy Fyvert. At least for some years it has been a sort of family arrangement about them. Just of late, however, I have begun to wonder whether it will ever come to anything. They seem to regard one another as cousins and Mr. Daventry certainly admires Miss Balmaine. This is being very confidential, Mr. Cardyn, but I wish you to be thoroughly *au courant* with everything in the house."

"I quite understand that," Cardyn said quietly. "But you said just now that every member of the household had a motive. I presume these young people are included?"

Lady Anne bent her head and for a moment pressed her dainty handkerchief to her lips.

"Every one in the house has some motive, as I said. By my husband's will, his private fortune— a very large one—is divided at my death between John Daventry and the heirs of my husband's daughter, Marjorie—Miss Balmaine, in other words. Should Mr. Daventry predecease me his share passes on with my estate. Oh, I was forgetting! Until last Saturday my house had another inmate—my secretary, David Branksome. Now, Mr. Cardyn, as I told you, I am looking for a new secretary, and it occurred to me that the post might be occupied by one of your employees who, while ostensibly working with me, might be really watching over my safety."

"A very good idea," Cardyn assented. "With your permission I will take the post myself. I suppose there are no special qualifications needed."

Lady Anne looked a little doubtful.

"I have a collection of wonderful old miniatures, which I am having catalogued and described. Do you know anything of them? Of course I could help you."

"I think I should be able to manage." Cardyn made an entry in his book. Then he looked at her, tapping his lips with his pencil as he waited. "May I ask why Mr. Branksome left?"

Lady Anne hesitated.

"I had some reason to be displeased with him," she said stiffly. "But that does not enter into this matter at all."

Bruce Cardyn frowned.

"Pardon me, I think it does. In that very cause for your displeasure may lie the clue to the mystery we are trying to solve. You must be perfectly frank with me, Lady Anne."

Lady Anne's indecision was apparent, but at last common-sense prevailed.

"Well, I do not see how it can have the slightest connection," she surrendered. "But, though David Branksome was in some respects a good enough secretary, I did not care for him; he took too much upon himself—I hardly know how to describe it— and I seriously objected to his manner with Miss Balmaine. She, of course, coming from Australia, where I suppose all men are equal, apparently saw no harm in it. She assured me that she had no thought of anything serious and begged me not to dismiss him, but I felt it best to keep to my resolution. But I think this is begging the question, Mr. Cardyn. David Branksome alone of my household was not mentioned in my will. He was only a recent acquisition called in to help me in cataloguing my collection of miniatures, and the old editions in the library downstairs. Thus he had no motive. And, moreover, he had left me before I discovered the eighth pill. No, he had certainly no motive."

"H'm! No. Nevertheless, I think I will look Mr. Branksome up a bit. There is no certainty, as far as can see, when the extra pill was added. Was he with you before Miss Balmaine came, Lady Anne?"

"Oh, yes. A couple of months, should think." Lady Anne wrinkled up her brows. "I can give you the exact dates by looking up my diary."

She drew the book at her side towards her and turned over the pages rapidly.

"Here it is! Branksome came to me on the 12th of September last year; Miss Balmaine reached us on the 29th of October."

"I see." Bruce Cardyn put the elastic band round his pocket-book. "Lady Anne, your new secretary would like to come in at once."

"To-day?" Lady Anne questioned.

"In an hour's time," Cardyn acquiesced. "I have to go back to the office to make a few arrangements. For, with your permission, I am going to set a watch on the house outside!"

"Outside?" Lady Anne raised her eyebrows. "Really, I do not think that is necessary, Mr. Cardyn. The outside staff have no possible means of access—"

"It is not so much the outside staff that I am thinking of, though I shall give them a little attention, too, but I want any communication that the people inside the house have with outsiders carefully watched. In some cases, too, there will be probably shadowing to be done. But you have given me carte blanche, Lady Anne, though I will not trouble you with the details of my precautions, I want you to feel that you are perfectly safe. For a few days I am going to ask you to eat only at meal-times, when there can be no certainty beforehand who will partake of the food. Eschew all odd cups of milk, even your morning tea, until the assassin is found. I will get your prescription made up at the chemist's myself, if you will permit, and give the medicines into your own hands. While you will, I hope, keep them all locked up and allow no one to have access to them."

"I dare say I can manage it," Lady Anne said doubtfully. "But I am afraid Pirnie will be offended. She is my confidential maid, you understand, and the most faithful, the most honest creature in the world. For me even to say that she is entirely beyond suspicion is absurd."

Bruce Cardyn coughed.

"Nevertheless, even the most confidential of maids must be suspect until we have discovered the guilty person. I must ask you to adhere strictly to this rule, please, Lady Anne."

"Well, well, leave it in your hands," Lady Anne conceded. "Only make me safe, though I dare say you are thinking it is an unnecessary bother to make about an old woman."

The detective got up.

"I will safeguard your life as I would have done my own mother's, Lady Anne."

He took a few steps up the room looking grave and preoccupied.

"Of course it is my duty to tell you that it is my opinion that the only way to make you absolutely safe is for you to leave this house, letting no one know where you go or how long you will be away, taking no one with you, and of course not returning until we have discovered the identity of the would-be assassin."

"Oh, I couldn't do that," Lady Anne said in her most positive tone. "My good man, I have long since given up going away for change of air, as they call it. I can get all the change of air that I want in London, and an invalid is best by her own fireside. So, if you cannot make me safe here—" Her gesture was expressive.

"I feel no doubt but that we shall be able to do so," Bruce Cardyn said quickly, "only I was bound to lay the other possibility before you."

Something like a grim smile passed over Lady Anne's countenance.

"Well, you have put it before me and I refuse to have anything to do with it; therefore the responsibility is off your shoulders. In an hour, then, I shall expect you, Mr. Cardyn. By the way, under what name shall you pass as my secretary?"

"Oh, Cardyn, please," the detective said at once. "Of course, in any mention of our work officially, we are called by the name of the firm, and even that is not as well-known to the criminal classes as I should like it to be."

"As you wish." Lady Anne touched the bell and the footman appeared to show Cardyn out.

The detective glanced at him keenly. "A young man from the country," he decided.

Soames, the butler, was hovering about in the hall, a be-nevolent-looking, elderly man, whose bland face and dignified, stately manner might have been those of a Bishop or a Minister of State.

Cardyn took a taxi back to his office. As he let himself in with a key his partner looked out of the adjoining room—a keen-faced, clean-shaven man, a few years older than Cardyn.

"Well!"

"Well!" Cardyn responded in a non-committal voice.

The other laughed.

"Is it to be you or me?"

"Me, I think!" Cardyn's voice was firm. "For the reason I told you I wish to undertake the work."

CHAPTER III

"Monsieur Melange is with her ladyship, sir."

"Monsieur Melange!" Bruce Cardyn repeated with a doubt-ful glance at Soames's placid face.

"The French gentleman to see the miniatures, sir," the but-ler went on, his manner as gravely respectful to the secretary as though the young man had been Squire Daventry himself. Soames's manners were always perfect. Somehow he conveyed the impression that they were something demanded by his self-respect, and quite irrespective of the person whom he was addressing.

"Yes, sir. His lordship and Lady Barminster are coming to lunch. They are coming over with Miss Fyvert and Mr. John Daventry."

"Is that so? Mr. Daventry is Squire Daventry of the Keep, isn't he?" Bruce questioned.

"Yes, sir. Though it seems strange to think of him there, and the old Squire and both his sons gone."

"Oh, well, times change and we change with them," Bruce said as he went on.

The butler looked after him with an indulgent smile. Bruce Cardyn in his character as secretary had been a week at the house in Charlton Crescent, and he appeared to be gaining

it was a sketch of a fair-haired girl in water-colours, who bore a striking resemblance to Miss Balmaine, and underneath was written in a clear masculine handwriting, with which he had become oddly familiar of late, "Daisy Melville, April, 19—"

It was only a glance he had as he went forward, while Maureen, with an angry exclamation sprang up trying to tear it from his hands.

"This is your property, I believe, Miss Balmaine," he said as he held it out over Maureen's head.

That young lady gave a howl of rage.

"I call that frightfully mean of you, Mr. Cardyn!"

She wriggled away from Cardyn and ran towards the door.

"Anyway, he had a good look at it before he gave it to you," she called back mischievously. "I believe he is in love with you, Margaret! He is always asking questions about you!"

Then, a most unusual thing with Bruce Cardyn, he suddenly lost his temper.

"Damn!" he exclaimed. "I beg your pardon, Miss Balmaine, but really that child—"

"Please say it again for me." Margaret Balmaine laughed. She had rapidly recovered her self-possession, though her breathing was still quickened, and her blue eyes were sparkling with anger. "Maureen is simply intolerable. Any language about her is excusable. Lady Anne ought really to get a holiday governess for her if she stays away from school. She is always about with the housemaid, Alice, which is not good for her. But I suspect she will be better when Dorothy is at home."

She broke off as Maureen came out again, clinging to the arm of a tall girl at sight of whom Bruce Cardyn rubbed his eyes in amazement. A tall girl in a long motoring coat, a pull-on hat over her chestnut-hair—hair which had been bobbed once and which was now allowed to curl at its own sweet will round the pretty smiling face with its brown eyes and its colour coming and going; and there was, in spite of the difference in everything—age, expression and colouring—a distinct likeness to Lady Anne.

The eyes opened wide now with an expression as astonished as those of Bruce Cardyn. She did not even glance at Miss Balmaine who had rolled up the sketch in her hand and was now coming towards her.

"You!" she exclaimed. "You!"

"You!" Bruce Cardyn echoed blankly. "I did not know that you—"

"I am Dorothy Fyvert." The girl held out her hands to him with a pretty welcoming gesture. "And you—"

"I am Bruce Cardyn—Lady Anne Daventry's secretary," the man interrupted as he bent low over the outstretched hands.

"But, Dorothy, Dorothy, do you know him?" Maureen burst in, shaking her sister's arm up and down in her excitement. "Because, when I told you I did not like him—not even as well as I had liked Mr. Branksome—you never said—"

Miss Fyvert touched her small sister rebukingly. "Hush! Maureen, darling. It is not at all kind to say you do not like people. And you will have to like Mr. Cardyn very much because he saved my life once!"

"O—h!" Maureen's eyes were wide with excitement now. "Dorothy, you don't mean—you can't mean that he is the man who climbed up and got you out of the fire!"

"At Lady Barminster's—yes!" Dorothy answered, her pretty eyes smiling at the young man. "How often I have wanted to thank you!" she went on. "It does seem strange that we should meet at last—here—like this!"

"It does, indeed!" Cardyn responded, thinking she little knew how strange.

"I am so glad—" Dorothy was beginning when she was interrupted by a cry from the house.

"Dorothy! Dorothy! where are you?"

"Here, here!" the girl called back. She smiled again at Cardyn. "At any rate I shall see you again soon. We shall not lose sight of one another now."

Cardyn saw that quite a crowd of young people seemed to take possession of her altogether.

He felt a curious sense of depression as he followed more slowly and made his way back to the little study where Monsieur Melange was still poring over the miniatures.

"Zis—zis, is very fine. I see too a likeness—a resemblance to ze Lady Anne," he said as Cardyn came in.

The younger man realized at once that some one was in Lady Anne's room. He sat down and hastily scribbled a line on a scrap of paper and handed it to Monsieur Melange.

"Find out as soon as possible what is known of the past of a young actress called Daisy Melville, probably playing in Sydney in the summer of last year."

CHAPTER IV

"THIS IS MY new secretary, John—Mr. Bruce Cardyn."

"How-d'ye-do." John Daventry shook hands heartily, as they sat down to the luncheon table.

Bruce Cardyn glanced keenly at the young man who was now taking the place opposite Lady Anne.

There was nothing very remarkable about John Daventry. He was just the ordinary well set-up, well-dressed young Englishman, with a rather unusually attractive expression, perhaps. Certainly no one could have looked less like a murderer, above all a secret poisoner, Bruce Cardyn decided as he studied the fair, regular features, the sunburnt skin telling of an outdoor life as the regular white teeth and bright dark eyes spoke of perfect health.

But Cardyn had been long enough in his chosen profession to know that nothing is more deceptive than the appearance. Some of the worst criminals have been handsome, pleasant-looking people, whose most important asset has been their charming manner. Wherefore he by no means crossed John Daventry off his list of suspects.

Dorothy Fyvert was sitting lower down the table on the same side as Cardyn. But it was noticeable that Daventry did not seem to have any glances to spare for her. Constantly his eyes wandered in the direction of his newly-found cousin, Margaret Balmaine. Miss Balmaine was opposite—all her attention apparently given to the man who sat next her and who had come with Lady Barminster.

Next to Lady Anne on one side was Monsieur Melange. Bruce Cardyn could hear him discussing miniatures with her and old Lady Barminster, Maureen was next to Cardyn himself. Quite evidently he had incurred her severe displeasure. He could see little but one hunched-up shoulder and the bright bobbed hair that was so like her sister's.

For a long time there was a perfect babel of conversation in which it was difficult to distinguish any one voice, but at last one clear young voice rang out above the others:

"Lady Anne, after lunch will you show us your pearls? Lady Barminster was telling us yesterday what magnificent jewels you had, amongst others a wonderful rope of pearls, that your father and mother gave you on your birthdays."

Lady Anne looked rather surprised.

"I do not often show my jewels. I do not often look at them myself," she said, slowly. "My jewel-wearing days are over. My pearls seldom see the light. They were given to me one by one by my parents. They began, I believe, on my very first birthday of all, and afterwards every Christmas and New Year as well as birthdays and other joyful occasions found my chain added to. My husband liked the idea and helped to carry it out. The old diamond and enamel clasp that fastens it was one of his wedding gifts to me. So, as you may imagine, my necklace is a fairly long one. But—"

There arose quite a chorus of exclamations. Everyone seemed to be talking at once, and all united at last in beseeching Lady Anne to show her pearls.

In some moods, the very outcry would have made Lady Anne determined to refuse, but to-day, it may be that the very peril in which she stood had moved her.

"We will go up to my sitting-room after lunch and I will show them to you," she promised.

"But you don't mean to say that you keep them in the house, Lady Anne?" old Lord Barminster remonstrated. "Damned dangerous thing to do. Ours are all at the Bank, and if my lady wants to make herself smart unexpectedly she has to put up with paste!" He ended with a chuckle that broke into a burst of coughing.

Lady Anne smiled serenely, but the curl of her upper lip betrayed the fact that the Barminster jewels had never been high in her estimation.

Bruce Cardyn alone sat silent. The mention of the pearls gave him new ground for thought. It did not seem that their presence in the house could have anything to do with the mystery he was there to investigate. They would certainly provide a motive for robbery or burglary, but secret poisoning was in a different category altogether. Yet, for all this conviction of his, he had a certain presentiment that the clue to the maze in which he was wandering had been placed in his hands, though at present he did not see how to make use of it. His eyes strayed to Monsieur Melange's mildly bored face; only miniatures appeared to interest that gentleman, and he was obviously waiting his opportunity to turn again to Lady Anne with his mild prattle of Coros and Lavellettos.

Cardyn himself was thinking over the problem of the jewels when an hour later he realized, from the merry chatter in Lady Anne's room, that her guests were keeping her to her word. Monsieur Melange had departed pleading another engagement immediately after lunch. Lord and Lady Barminster with certain of their guests had gone on their way wishing to make the most of the daylight, so that only John Daventry and a couple of girls the Barminsters had brought with them remained.

Cardyn had purposely left the communicating door ajar and presently he heard Lady Anne call out:

"You there, Mr. Cardyn? I am going to turn all these noisy young people in to you while I get my pearls out. I don't care that the secret that guards them should be known to every one. People may be all right by themselves, but their associates may be burglars or the Lord knows who!"

"My dear Aunt Anne, what a lurid imagination you have, or have you been taking a course of detective novels?" John Daventry laughed as he held the door open for the girls.

They all came across to the table where Cardyn had been working and began to admire the miniatures.

John Daventry did not pretend to be much interested.

"We have drawers full of them at the Keep," he said. "But I would almost as soon have a lot of old photographs. If you don't know the people, what good are they?"

"What a Goth you are, John!" Dorothy laughed as she bent over the tray. "It must be most absorbing work, Mr. Cardyn."

"It is rather," Bruce assented, his brows contracting as he noticed how John Daventry's eyes followed every movement of Margaret Balmaine, and how his voice softened as he spoke to her. Was Dorothy Fyvert to be slighted for this girl? And yet—Cardyn himself had hardly realized until he met her again how the memory of Dorothy Fyvert had haunted his dreams since that night, two years ago, when he brought her out of the burning house in his arms—how often he had recalled her sweet brown eyes, with their long up-curling lashes, her pretty hair, bobbed then, now attempting to grow again and curling at its own sweet will all over her small head.

But of what use was it for a poor detective to dream of Lady Anne Daventry's niece? He gave himself a shake, called himself a blockhead, and, disregarding John Daventry's black looks, went over to Miss Balmaine who was standing by the window looking into the garden. She welcomed him with a bright smile. A man is always a man to a woman of Margaret Balmaine's type.

Bruce Cardyn smiled too. He was anxious just at the present to get on friendly terms with Margaret Balmaine, to have a little private conversation with her, and hitherto he had not been able to find an opportunity. He did not see how Dorothy Fyvert's eyes followed him, a wistful look in their brown depths. Was he, too, to fall a victim to this strange girl's fascination?

"Any more encounters with Maureen, Miss Balmaine?" he questioned lightly.

The girl shook her head.

"Not yet, I am glad to say. I have not your command of language, you see!" she said demurely.

"It might be acquired," he suggested.

"Fancy Lady Anne's wrath if it were." Miss Balmaine laughed. "Seriously, though, I find Maureen a most disturbing element in the house. She is not really obedient to Dorothy. And she is always racing about with one of the housemaids, as I told you, and I don't think it improves her."

"I don't suppose it does," Cardyn acquiesced. "Still, I dare say a little running wild won't hurt the child. She has such high spirits that she must find being cooped up in school very trying."

"And other people find it very trying when she isn't," Miss Balmaine said petulantly.

"I dare say they do," Bruce agreed. "I hear you come from Sydney, Miss Balmaine."

The girl did not look pleased at the sudden change of subject.

"Not from Sydney," she said shortly. "My home was many miles away."

"You must have had a very interesting life out there," Cardyn went on. "I have often meant to go out to Australia. I have even thought of settling down there, but something has always stood in the way."

"You have never been there?" the girl questioned.

He hesitated a moment.

"Well, I have. As a matter of fact I was born there, but I was brought home when I was too young to have properly appreciated my birthplace. Still, I suppose—" he shrugged his shoulders—"it may be because it is my birthplace that it appeals to me."

Margaret Balmaine's face altered indefinably.

"Where were you born?"

"In Melbourne, I believe," Bruce lied. "But my parents moved up-country and took a sheep farm there. They did not make it pay—in fact, lost all their money. Still, Miss Balmaine—"

He was interrupted by a sharp cry from the sitting-room.

"Mr. Cardyn! Mr. Cardyn! Come!"

It was Lady Anne's voice.

Hardly knowing what he feared, Bruce sprang to the intervening door and flung it open. Lady Anne was standing before her escritoire as if she had pulled herself up in her agitation. Her face was towards them, and it was white; the fear in her eyes that Bruce had seen on his first visit had deepened. Her left hand with the great diamond flashing over her wedding ring was grasping the top of the escritoire, and shaking as it clasped, so that in the momentary silence that followed her cry the two who were first in the room, Bruce Cardyn and John Daventry, could hear the rattling of the various objects that always stood before Lady Anne on the writing flap.

"My pearls! John! Mr. Cardyn!" she cried, as the two men caught her arms and helped her back to her chair. "My pearls have gone!"

"Impossible!" John Daventry began. "You must have put them somewhere else."

"When did you see them last?" Bruce Cardyn's voice cut across the other's, cool and incisive.

"About a month ago." Lady Anne's voice was firm and as controlled as ever now. She sat up and put John Daventry's arm from her. "I am not a fool to make a mistake about a thing of that kind. I remember exactly when I saw them and remember thinking that the clasp was loose and must be seen to."

"Where did you keep them?" Cardyn questioned.

For answer Lady Anne pointed to the escritoire. The door in the middle stood open and Cardyn saw that the back was a sliding panel after the fashion of those beloved of the Florentine makers. Behind it was an aperture, large, comparing it with the size of the escritoire; inside were several cases—one lay in front of Lady Anne on the flap. It was open and empty.

"You see," said Lady Anne. "The last time I had that case out the pearls were there. Now they are gone in spite of all my precautions. And—"

She paused. Cardyn and Daventry peered into the open cavity. The girls stood in the doorway huddled together in a frightened fashion.

"Oh, Aunt Anne! It can't be true! But I don't believe they can have been stolen—your lovely pearls! You must have put them somewhere else," Dorothy cried, while Margaret Balmaine looked on in horrified dismay.

"Put them somewhere else, indeed," Lady Anne said with a snort of contempt. "Are you a fool, child, or do you take me for one? I tell you, I put the pearls in there myself a month ago with all the usual precautions, and they have been taken away. Not by a burglar or a thief. No lock or spring has been broken. All have been unfastened and fastened again without any sign that a strange hand has touched them. Some one has learned the secret of the safe and used it, and has also got hold of my keys."

"Did absolutely no one know this secret but yourself, Lady Anne?" Bruce Cardyn questioned in an authoritative tone that made John Daventry look at him in surprise.

"Absolutely no one," Lady Anne cried emphatically.

"Your maid?"

"Knows no more than anyone else," Lady Anne answered, her eyes glancing from the detective to John Daventry, from him again to the group of girls in the doorway.

"Carry your memory back, Lady Anne, and see if you can recall any incident, however slight, that might have given anyone an inkling of the secret spring," Cardyn said again. "Sometimes a word is dropped that might be interpreted by some one on the look-out, or a letter—"

"Neither written nor spoken word has been dropped by me," Lady Anne declared with decision. "Still, I suppose there are burglars clever enough to set any precautions at naught." And as she spoke her keen eyes were watching, searching all the faces around.

"It would be a clever burglar who found the pearls in their hiding-place without help, and took them away without leaving any trace," Cardyn said quickly. "The other cases in the escritoire, Lady Anne. Have you looked whether their contents are safe?"

"No." Lady Anne leaned forward and opened one. "This is all right. I expect they all are. There is nothing of any value there—there has been nothing but the pearls for some months. Fortunately I moved my diamonds and all my rings, except the one I always wear some time ago, to the Bank—rings are out of place on crippled hands and knuckles swollen by arthritis. So they are all safe and the thieves have not had so big a haul as they expected."

"Nevertheless, my dear aunt, in spite of that they have had a remarkably good haul in taking several thousand pounds' worth of pearls." John Daventry looked at Cardyn who was searching the hiding-place in the escritoire as though he thought the young man was taking too much upon himself. "Scotland Yard must be called in at once," he went on. "It is quite useless for amateurs to make suggestions."

"Quite!" Lady Anne agreed in her clear, crisp tones. "Do not trouble, John, I shall consult the police as soon as possible. Mercy on us! What is this?"

"This" was a loud wail that was set up from the doorway. Some one appeared to be going into hysterics.

"It is Pirnie, Lady Anne," said Margaret Balmaine. The girl looked frightened to death, her make-up standing out in ghastly contrast with the pallor of her face. "She was going by and I told her your pearls were missing."

Lady Anne could not suppress an expression of impatience.

"I wish you had held your tongue, Margaret. Don't be an hysterical fool, Pirnie!" she said, raising her voice. "If I do not weep and lament surely you need not."

"Oh, my lady, my lady! I can't get over it," the woman wailed as she pushed herself in front of Dorothy Fyvert.

Bruce Cardyn looked at her curiously. She was the one member of the household of whom he had hitherto seen the least. She was a tall, rather affected-looking woman evidently verging on middle-age, while clinging with both hands to the last vestige of youth. She still retained the remains of early good looks.

"I can't believe it, my lady! Your lovely pearls gone, that I have always been so proud of. I have always wanted you to put them in the Bank, your ladyship knows, and now I suppose everybody will be saying that I have taken them, though I'm as innocent as a babe unborn."

"Now may Heaven grant me patience with a fool!" Lady Anne groaned in her exasperation. "Please wait to protest your innocence until you are accused, Pirnie!"

CHAPTER V

"DETECTIVE INSPECTOR Furnival will be here as soon as possible," Lady Anne announced.

She had come into the small study where Bruce Cardyn was working, walking with her stick as usual, and disdaining all proffered help. She waited before closing the door, and spoke apparently for the benefit of those behind her:

"I wish you to receive him, Mr. Cardyn, and to do what you can to help him."

Then she shut the door very carefully and came forward totteringly to the chair the young man placed for her.

"Well?" she said interrogatively. "Is this robbery of the pearls connected with the work you have in hand?"

Bruce Cardyn shrugged his broad shoulders.

"I don't quite see the connexion, Lady Anne, since, if the thief were already in possession of the pearls, it is difficult to understand why he should wish you out of the way."

"Unless he—or she," Lady Anne said very deliberately, "wished to possess himself—or herself—of the diamonds."

"And that, as they were at the Bank, he was hardly likely to do," Bruce remarked. "Unless they came to him by inheritance. And Mr. Daventry—"

"Mr. Daventry will not inherit my diamonds," Lady Anne said sharply. "I have left them to my niece, Miss Dorothy Fyvert."

"Then that settles the question of any connexion, of course," Bruce said indignantly.

"Naturally it does," Lady Anne agreed with a far-away look in her eyes. "Well, Mr. Cardyn, it is no use your or my spending time in guessing. What I came to you to say is, I wish no faintest hint of the work you are really here to do to reach Inspector Furnival's ears, until I give you permission."

Bruce sat silent for a moment.

"That will be extremely difficult, Lady Anne! Inspector Furnival does not know me personally, it is true, but he is sure to discover who am, and then how am to account for my presence here?"

"I do not care, you must invent something," Lady Anne said in her most autocratic manner. "What is the good of your being a detective if you cannot?"

"It seems to me," Cardyn went on, "that the two cases are so interwoven that he would find the knowledge a help in his task."

"I do not care about that," Lady Anne snapped. Then, her manner growing more impressive, "Don't you understand, Mr. Cardyn, that I called you in instead of the regular police because, when you have discovered my would-be murderer, I may wish the whole affair hushed up—-for the sake of my family?" Her voice sank to a whisper and she got up, carefully averting her eyes from Bruce Cardyn's face.

He got up too, and mechanically offered her his arm, one conclusion forcing itself upon him—"Then she has some suspicion after all! But who?"

It was not an hour yet since the loss of the pearls had been discovered, and had thrown the usually peaceful household at the house in Charlton Crescent in a ferment. Bruce Cardyn and John Daventry had searched the escritoire together carefully, but had found no trace of the missing jewels and had only made themselves certain of what Lady Anne had said at first— the locks and springs that guarded the pearls had not been tampered with. Everything had been opened and reclosed in the ordinary way. Some one had found out the secret of the escritoire—but who? It seemed difficult to imagine that anyone outside the house could have had an opportunity of doing so.

From the moment of her outburst, Cardyn had had an uneasy feeling that Pirnie had known more than she acknowledged, though he realized that he had not the slightest real ground for his suspicion except the knowledge that she must have had many more opportunities of watching Lady Anne when she put away the pearls or got them out. There was something about Pirnie's face that he did not like too, and he had fancied that her dramatic outburst when she heard of the loss of the pearls did not ring quite true.

Lady Anne, however, evidently resented his suspicions of her maid, who appeared to be the only person in whose profession of affection she had any faith. Pirnie had insisted on searching in every likely and unlikely place for the pearls since their loss had been found out, and Cardyn had kept her as much as possible under observation.

Already the short January twilight was creeping on, and Bruce Cardyn was about to switch on the electric light when the door opened and Margaret Balmaine put her head in.

"Why, how miserable you look here, Mr. Cardyn! No lights and the fire out? We have at least got a good fire in Lady Anne's sitting-room, and Lady Anne says you are to come in and have some tea. We must try and pull ourselves together even if the pearls are lost. Soames has brought us up some lovely hot scones. He is doing all the waiting himself, just as if it were a wedding or a funeral!"

"Poor old Soames! A butler always feels most at home at one of the above-mentioned ceremonies, I fancy," Cardyn said as he followed her. But though he spoke with apparent lightness his eyes had never been keener or more alert than now, as he glanced from one to the other of the little group round the fire in Lady Anne's sitting-room.

Lady Anne herself was sitting near the escritoire in her revolving chair; Dorothy Fyvert was busy at the tea-table; and John Daventry stood on the hearthrug waiting to hand round the hot cakes. By the flickering light of the flames as they leaped up Cardyn could see that every face looked white and troubled. Lady Anne's was the most unmoved of them all; her hands, with their rheumatic knuckles were resting on the open flap of the escritoire before her. Every now and then her eyes wandered curiously round, and Cardyn guessed that she was asking herself whether it was—whether it could be possible that one of these dear familiar people had robbed her of her pearls and, not content with despoiling her, was further encompassing her death?

A great pang of pity for her loneliness shot through him. The death of her boys had left her bereft indeed, and she had turned her hardest side to the world ever since, but he guessed that the apparent hardness covered a kind and loyal heart.

Various odd pieces of jewellery were lying about the room on the Victorian centre-table and on the flap of the writing-table. Lady Anne smiled as she saw Bruce looking at them.

"Various treasures that Pirnie had unearthed in her zeal that no possible place of hiding for the pearls should be overlooked," she remarked. "Of no value, most of them. This is the only thing that is worth much—a dagger." And she reached out her hand and picked up a short slender blade set in a gold and jewelled handle. "That was given to my father when he was in India by one of the native princes. It is said to be worth something fabulous."

"Yes, I remember seeing this when I was a boy," John Daventry said as he came forward and weighed it in his hand. "A nice sort of toy. I expect you would be a match for a whole army of burglars with this, Aunt Anne. You wouldn't lose any more pearls if the thieves knew you were armed with this."

"Well, I haven't any more pearls to lose," Lady Anne said in her most matter-of-fact tones. "And, if I had, I am sure my poor rheumatic hands would not be able to defend them. Where is Maureen, Dorothy?"

"She has been out for a walk with Alice. They seem to have some great secret together to-day." Miss Fyvert answered. "And I believe she is having tea with Alice too. I am quite out of favour with her, and I fancy she is sulking because I would not talk to her about the pearls. She is such an excitable child, and quite fond enough of talking about robbers and burglars as it is. She is very fond of Alice too."

"Too fond, I think," Miss Balmaine said significantly. "She would not be allowed to be so much with the servants if she were my sister. I should get a temporary governess for her until she goes back to school."

"I am afraid we shall have to do something of the sort," said Dorothy absently. "But Maureen will hate it so, and Alice is quite a nice girl. Cream, Mr. Cardyn, and sugar?"

"No cream, please. But sugar—heaps of it—three lumps at least," Bruce said as he strode up to take his cup from her hand. "How this Russian fashion of taking lemon in tea grows. It wouldn't do for me."

"Nor for me either," Dorothy laughed. "I am a sugar-baby too. Oh, Soames, how lovely! You do spoil us!" as the butler entered the room with a tray of hot cakes in his hand.

"Only the spoiling is unnecessary as the last lot is not finished yet," John Daventry said, helping himself to another piece of cake.

Soames regarded him benevolently.

"They don't last long, sir. I know the young ladies' tastes. If Miss Maureen—Ah!"

The covered dish which he was about to set upon the tea-table dropped from his hand and he stood still, staring at the window farthest from Lady Anne. His breath came quick and fast, his jaws worked about from side to side. Everyone turned to look, and there was an outburst of screams from the girls. Then Bruce Cardyn sprang forward.

Outside the window, so close to the pane that it seemed to be pressing against it, was a white face—a chalk-white face, whether of man or woman none could tell. Around it there seemed to float a grey mist. Spirit or living creature! Even Bruce Cardyn, keen-witted detective as he was, felt a momentary doubt. He shook the window. It was latched. As he raised his hand to open it he momentarily took his eyes from the figure outside, and in that moment it vanished. Throwing the sash up he leaned out, conscious that the others were pressing up against him, calling, questioning, exclaiming.

Hearing the outcry, a man came running across the grass towards the house. Cardyn was rubbing his eyes in utter amazement; where on earth had the figure at the window disappeared to? What in the world had become of it? There was no ladder or rope to be seen, no sign of anyone on the terrace beneath. And yet Bruce had only taken his eyes off the creature, whatever it was, for one moment, not time enough for the slickest burglar to have got away.

The man hastening over the lawn had reached the sundial at the foot of the low terrace now—Cardyn knew him for one of his underlings, put on as an extra gardener to watch the house.

"Bradley!" he shouted. "Some one has been trying to get into the house and pretty nearly succeeded too. Did you see him?"

"No, sir!" said the man, staring upwards in a puzzled fashion, "leastways, just as I heard the shouting I thought I saw something moving on the wall, but didn't notice where it came from or where it went to. I don't think it was a man—all gliding about like a snake it was."

"Snakes haven't got white faces," Cardyn said sharply.

"The Cat Burglar!" One of the girls behind him cried out.

Cardyn never knew which, for in the pause which followed, his quick ear caught another sound—a groan, a cry, a stifled choking groan.

"What was that?" he cried, turning quickly and pushing back those who were pressing against him—John Daventry, Margaret Balmaine, Dorothy Fyvert and Soames.

Nobody answered him. Every one appeared to be struggling to lean out of the window at once.

With a terrible prevision of evil, he extricated himself from the crush. The next minute he knew that his prevision had been horribly justified. Lady Anne sat still in her revolving chair, but she had fallen aside and lay across the arm in a huddled-up position. It was from her lips that cry had come—they were still parted, open, and from one corner a thin stream of blood and froth was trickling down her chin on to the laces of her gown.

As Cardyn reached her she opened her eyes and looked at him with a gleam of comprehension.

"It was—it was—"

The last word broke in a rush of blood. Lady Anne's head fell back, her jaw dropped, and before anyone could realize the horror that had happened in their midst the keen-witted, clear-headed mistress of the house in Charlton Crescent had ceased to exist. For one moment he thought of heart failure—of an aneurism that had burst crossed Cardyn's mind. Then in a flash he realized— knew that what he had sworn to prevent had happened. In spite of all his precautions Lady Anne's assassin had been successful. But now John Daventry and Soames were beside him. They cried aloud in horror; they tried to raise Lady Anne but she lay in their arms a limp, inert mass.

"It is her heart—it has been weak for years! That brute has killed her—the shock of seeing him at the window has frightened her to death!"

"Shock had nothing to do with it," Cardyn said shortly. He motioned Soames aside and took the pitiful-looking figure that till ten minutes ago had been the masterful Lady Anne Daventry from John Daventry. He rested it as well as he could against the wooden back of a chair.

"Look!" he cried, pointing downwards.

Protruding from the dead woman's breast was the gold and jewelled dagger she had shown them half an hour before. And, looking horribly incongruous among the laces of her fichu, a deep stain was spreading.

Some one had switched on the electric light and Cardyn saw that John Daventry's ruddy face had turned an ugly, sickly green, that Dorothy Fyvert and Margaret Balmaine were clinging together, shaking with fright—even in that awful moment his eyebrows contracted at the sight—and that Soames stood staring at his dead mistress like a man turned to stone. But as Bruce looked at him his face twitched to one side, and he put up his hands.

"Oh, my poor lady! my poor lady!"

"But what does it mean—what has happened?" John Daventry demanded, his voice and manners those of a man out of his mind.

For answer Cardyn pointed to the handle of the dagger—to that ominous growing stain.

"Murder!" he said laconically. "Wilful murder!"

CHAPTER VI

"I CAN'T BELIEVE IT! I can't believe it!" John Daventry reiterated, pressing his handkerchief over his brow.

He had been saying the same thing at intervals ever since Cardyn had literally pushed him out of the chamber of death. For in her sitting-room Lady Anne still sat in death, where she had so often sat in life, the eternal question that her eyes had asked of late answered at last—for her!

For the rest of them it had become a thousand times more insistent, more acute. As Bruce Cardyn glanced round at the faces of those who so short a time before had met in Lady Anne's sitting-room for tea, he saw the same question in the eyes of each—Who? Which?

Already they were beginning to draw shudderingly away from one another. Even the two girls, instead of clinging together, were eyeing one another furtively, shivering as each sat back in her chair.

Bruce Cardyn and John Daventry were standing in the middle of the room. The shock of the horror seemed almost to have scared Daventry's wits away.

Bruce Cardyn had been literally forced to take command of the situation. He it was who had insisted on the room being left exactly as it was until the arrival of the doctor and the police. He it was who had shepherded them all into the small library until they had been questioned.

The only addition to their number had been Pirnie, Lady Anne's maid, who knelt with her head against the sitting-room door, moaning and crying and calling upon her dead mistress by name.

Soames stood by the other door. As far as outward appearances went he was the attentive butler still, though a close observer would have noticed that his hands were shaking, that his eyes looked dull and strained. Even Bruce Cardyn, hardened detective though he was, had had his nerves shaken by the shock of Lady Anne's terrible death. He looked keenly at John Daventry now.

"Your belief, or non-belief, does not affect the situation unfortunately, Mr. Daventry. Lady Anne has been foully done to death in her own house and in our midst, and her murderer has to be found and punished whoever he may be."

John Daventry ran his hand through his hair. Though his face had somewhat recovered its ordinary colour, the sickly, greenish hue had not wholly disappeared.

"It—Of course I know that Lady Anne is dead," he said, with a little stammer between his words of which he had never been conscious before. "Dead! Murdered! That is horrible enough, Heaven knows. But you say—you said—"

"I say now what the world will probably say later," interrupted Bruce Cardyn, "that Lady Anne may have been murdered by one of the five people in the room."

"But how could it have been one of us?" Daventry stared at him again. "Myself, yourself, Soames, the two girls—could one of us have murdered her? Would any of us have murdered her?"

"Could anyone else have murdered her?" Bruce counter-questioned pithily.

"The doors were not locked," John Daventry said, looking at Soames. "Somebody might have rushed in from the outside."

"Yes. I have thought of that, sir," Soames interposed shakily. "If the assassin had been in concealment outside—"

"Or that brute at the window?" Daventry went on. "I believe myself he did it by some devilry or other. I don't profess to know how."

"It would be an impossibility," Bruce said shortly. The face at the window was puzzling him more than he would have cared to confess. "We were all at the open window looking for him. How could he have got in?"

"I don't know," Daventry said moodily. "He seemed to vanish. Where did he go anyway? As likely into that room as anywhere else I should say."

Bruce shook his head.

"He couldn't have come in through the window while we were all looking out of it. The other window nearest Lady Anne was closed."

"The window by her ladyship wasn't quite closed, sir," Soames corrected. "Her ladyship," with a brave attempt to swallow down a rising sob, "always had it left open a couple of inches at the top, for ventilation like."

"That wouldn't—"

Cardyn broke off. Steps were coming along the corridor. He opened the door. Two men came up to him, one whose profession was clearly stamped upon his clean-shaven face, its expression of geniality for once overclouded. The other—a very familiar face and figure to Bruce Cardyn—was Inspector Furnival of Scotland Yard, a thin man of middle height, still considerably on the sunny side of fifty.

*

"And that is all you can tell me, Mr. Cardyn?"

Inspector Furnival of Scotland Yard was the speaker. He sat at the head of the table in the dining-room in Lady Daventry's house in Charlton Crescent. He was rather unlike the ordinary detective of fiction in that he was small and alert-looking. His sharp inquisitive-looking little face had earned him the sobriquet of "The Ferret," when he was lower down in the Force, and the name stuck to him still. But there was many a crook who had learned to dread the Ferret's gimlet-like grey eyes more than he dreaded anything on earth.

Those same grey eyes were fixed on Bruce Cardyn's now, as if they would force the truth out of him. The younger detective was seated a little lower down the table where the clear light from a French window fell full upon his face.

"Absolutely everything," he said, meeting the inspector's eyes steadily. "It seems inconceivable, but—"

"But you and I have learnt that there is nothing inconceivable, Mr. Cardyn," the other interrupted. "Now, just let me run over my notes. You and Mr. Daventry, and the two girls were at tea with Lady Anne; the butler brought a tray in, and at the same moment a sixth person appeared at the window furthest from Lady Anne. You all rushed to the window, opened it, looked for the man outside. He had apparently disappeared.

You heard a groan, and when you turned you found Lady Anne dead, stabbed to the heart with her own dagger."

Bruce nodded.

"Quite correct!"

"And the inference you have drawn, I gather, is that the crime was committed by one of the people in the room."

Bruce looked at him.

"Is it not unavoidable?"

The inspector's eyes were gazing out into the garden with an abstracted far-away look just now.

"Not quite, think," he said gently. "How long were you at the window, Mr. Cardyn?"

"I should think about three minutes," Bruce said thoughtfully. "We were all so puzzled, or, speaking for myself, I should say I was so puzzled by the disappearance of the face at the window, that I signalled to one of my men who was walking about and watching the house from the outside to know what he had seen of him."

"And—" the inspector prompted.

"And he fancied he had seen something move in the ivy. But certainly no man had come down."

"Supposing he had gone up?" Inspector Furnival suggested.

Bruce shook his head.

"I thought of the roof at once, and looked up as well as down, but there was no one to be seen. As a matter of fact getting up to the roof at all in that fashion would be an impossibility-—even for the most expert climber. The ivy gets much thinner when it gets past the second floor, and stops altogether far short of the roof."

There was a pause. Inspector Furnival was drumming with his fingers on the table. Bruce Cardyn sat silent and motionless. His face was grave and troubled. From the moment her summons reached him, the case of Lady Anne Daventry had intrigued him as nothing else had done during his career as a detective. He had felt so hopeful, so certain of being able to safeguard Lady Anne, and to discover her would-be murderer. And never before had he failed so signally.

At last the inspector spoke again.

"I notice that you speak of the 'face at the window,' never of the 'man.'"

"No," Bruce acknowledged. "Because from my own observation I could not say whether it was a man or a woman. It was just like a chalk-white face with staring eyes and a mass of black hair. There seemed to be a kind of vague, intangible mist round it. That is all I can say."

"And a very queer 'all' it is too," the inspector remarked. "Now was it a real man or woman at all? Or was it—could it have been an illusion caused by some arrangement of lights—thrown on the window?"

"Not by any that I have heard of," Bruce said at once. "No. The face looked solid enough. Besides, what reason could anyone have for—"

"Why, they might want to do exactly what really happened. To divert your attention while the murder was committed," the inspector proceeded, his grey eyes looking here, there and everywhere except at the young man's face, and yet somehow noting every change of expression that flitted over it. "Might not that man, face, illusion, whatever it was, have been arranged for by someone who was waiting outside the door until the opportunity came? From what the butler says the door was not even shut."

Cardyn's face did not look responsive.

"Lady Anne was stabbed with her own dagger. No outsider could have arranged for that to have been found close at hand."

"That might have been seized when the murderer got there. He may have intended to use some other weapon, and been quick to see the advantage that using her own dagger would give him."

"Yes, he would have had to be quick indeed!" Bruce asserted satirically.

There was another pause. Both men were listening intently.

Though barely two hours had elapsed since Lady Anne's death, already it seemed to Cardyn that a lifetime had passed away. Inspector Furnival on the point of setting out for Charlton Crescent, had had his steps quickened by telephone. The doctor had been summoned in hot haste, but nothing could be done. The body had been moved to the couch, so that Dr. Spencer could make his brief examination, otherwise nothing in the room had been touched. The very teacups and saucers the members of Lady Anne's party had been using when Soames's cry startled them all still stood as they had hastily set them down.

At last there came the sound for which they had been waiting—a sharp knock at the door. At the same moment the passionate weeping of a woman reached them—"Oh, my lady! my lady!"

"Pirnie—Lady Anne's maid." Bruce Cardyn got up. "The woman is absolutely useless. That is all she can do—she simply cries all the time. Dr. Spencer is at the door, think."

The inspector motioned him to wait.

"Yes, Dr. Spencer is coming to report to us. But first I must put one question to you, Mr. Cardyn. You were the first at the window, you say. Of the other four people in the room was there anyone else close to you all the time, so that you can confidently say 'This one could not have been the murderer.'"

"They all seemed to be close to me all the time," Cardyn said ruefully. "Pressing me hard, so that I could scarcely move, you understand. But I could not say that any one of them was by me all the time. The one who seemed to be perhaps the longest—"

"Yes?" The inspector looked at him closely.

"Well, it was, think, Mr. John Daventry," Bruce finished. "But I could not be certain of all the time. Still, he was beside me shouting to the man below a good deal of the time, it seems to me. At the end, when I turned after hearing the groan, I recollect pushing Soames, the butler, back. But I do not remember where Mr. Daventry was then."

"John Daventry—um!" mused the inspector. "The heir, the most obvious trail, but is it the right one?"

"I don't know," Bruce Cardyn confessed. "He doesn't look like a murderer, but—"

"No one ever does look like a murderer until he is found out," the inspector said sententiously. "My experience is that people who look like murderers may be great philanthropists or prominent politicians, but they never commit murders. Well, doctor"—as Cardyn opened the door and Dr. Spencer came into the room—"what have you to say to us?"

The doctor was a capable-looking man of middle age, with a pleasant professional manner. Just now his face was white and disturbed.

"Us!" he repeated, raising his eyebrows as he glanced at Cardyn.

"Ah, yes! I had forgotten. Now this must be strictly in confidence, doctor. Mr. Bruce Cardyn, a member of one of the best-known firms of private detectives, is here at Lady Anne's own request, acting as her secretary, in order to discover, if possible, her secret enemy in the house."

The doctor stared at him.

"But what—I don't understand—Do you mean that Lady Anne—?"

"Feared that what happened this afternoon might happen?" the inspector finished. "Exactly! But you must understand that this must go no further, doctor. Mr. Cardyn must remain the secretary to the rest of the world. Now, what have you to tell us?"

"Nothing you do not know already," the doctor said slowly. "Leaving technicalities to the inquest, Lady Anne died of the wound caused by the dagger which was still in it when I came. It penetrated to the heart and death must have taken place within a few minutes. The blow must have been one of great force and should say struck by a person who knew just where to strike. That is all can tell you, inspector, and it will not help you much, fear."

"One never knows," the inspector said enigmatically. "One question, Dr. Spencer—you say 'a powerful blow.' Could it have been struck by a woman?"

"It depends upon the woman," the doctor said after a pause. "But, yes—I should say that in these days of athletic women most of them are as capable of striking hard as a man. But you surely do not think that—that a woman—"

"I am not thinking anything at present," Inspector Furnival interrupted. "I am trying to find out the truth, doctor."

"Quite so, I understand that. But there is one thing that has struck me might be a means of ascertaining the truth." The doctor laid his hat and stick on the table. "I am a bit of a criminologist myself, and in reading both real and imaginary accounts of crime it has struck me how very often finger-prints have been the means of tracking down the criminal. Now in this case, surely the dagger—the handle I mean, must bear the marks of—"

Something like a faint smile flitted momentarily over the inspector's face.

"I have not neglected what certainly does look like an obvious clue, doctor. But unfortunately so many people have handled the dagger, incidentally, Lady Anne herself, that I am afraid that it will not carry us much further."

"Ah, well! It is your job not mine." The doctor took up his hat. "I am more grieved than I can say that such a thing should have occurred. Lady Anne was one of my oldest patients and I shall miss her more than I can realize at present. And I trust that so cruel a crime will not long go unavenged. Well, if there is nothing more that I can tell you, inspector—we shall meet at the inquest to-morrow."

When the door had closed behind him the inspector made a rapid note in his book.

"Not very enlightening, that gentleman, now for Mr. John Daventry!"

John Daventry kept them waiting for some little time. The inspector occupied himself in studying his notes and adding a few words, his face gloomy and abstracted. Bruce Cardyn did not move. He was going over and over again the tragedy of this afternoon. Who could be guilty? Was it one of the four people in the room with him, or could it possibly have been, as the inspector suggested, some outsider? The face at the window too! Rack his brains as he would he could think of no explanation of this, to him the most inexplicable feature of the whole affair. With all the precautions he had taken it would have seemed an actual impossibility that anyone should have got up to the window of Lady Anne's room without being discovered at once. Yet the thing had happened.

John Daventry's face still bore evident marks of disturbance when at last he appeared.

"You asked for me, inspector?"

The inspector pointed to a chair next to Bruce Cardyn.

"Do you mind sitting there, Mr. Daventry?"

"Oh, I can't sit down, thanks."

Yet under the inspector's compelling eye, John Daventry walked over and laid his hand on the chair indicated.

"As a matter of fact you were lucky to catch me at all. The car will be round in a minute to take me to Daventry Keep. I want to break the news to my mother myself."

The inspector's hand still pointed to the chair.

"I think not, Mr. Daventry. You must let some one else break the news to them at the Keep. Don't you understand that no one—*no one* may leave this house without my permission?"

John Daventry stared at him.

"No one may leave this house without your permission!" he repeated contemptuously. "My good man, are you going out of your mind? I know that you police have a very exalted idea of your own powers. But really—"

The inspector pushed back his chair and stood up.

"You do not seem to comprehend at all the gravity of the situation, Mr. Daventry. A foul and terrible murder has been committed in this house this afternoon, and up till now we have entirely failed to trace the guilty one. In these circumstances every one of the five in the room must be suspect. All of them are under observation and should any one of them attempt to leave the house without my permission, he—or she—will at once be placed under arrest."

"I can't believe it!" That curious sickly pallor was stealing over John Daventry's face again. "You can't seriously think that one of us stabbed Aunt Anne? The very idea would be ludicrous if it were not so tragic."

"What do you think yourself, Mr. Daventry?" The Ferret's eyes had never been more gimletlike.

"I can't think." John Daventry ran his hands through his short hair. "But the idea that it was any one of us is inconceivable. The two girls must be out of the question, and I would trust Soames with my life any day. It must have been that blighter at the window, I said so at once."

The inspector's eyes did not relax their watchful gaze for a moment.

"You are talking of an impossibility, Mr. Daventry. The man could not have got through the window while you were all looking out."

Daventry stirred impatiently.

"Not at that window, of course he couldn't. But the other one—nearest to Aunt Anne—was open at the top. Soames says she would always have it so. The fellow must have managed it somehow through that. Oh, I don't pretend to say exactly how. But there is this chap, the Cat Burglar the papers have been full of lately, and how he has got up the most impossible looking walls. They say he has clamps on his feet, don't you know, or something of that kind—makes him stick to a flat surface like a fly. And those little beggars can walk upside-down on the ceiling."

The inspector did not appear to be particularly impressed by this fact in natural history.

"He would have needed clamps on his hands too, I fancy, to get through that window, stab Lady Anne and get back without any of you seeing him. No, Mr. Daventry, we shall have to think of some more likely story than that."

"Look here!" John Daventry started up. "Mr. Inspector Furnival, or whatever you call yourself, it strikes me that you are trying to be offensive. The police are always making mistakes, and you will find you have made a pretty big one if you don't take care. An Englishman's house is his castle, you know. And it would not take much to make me put you out of this neck and crop, detective inspector or not."

The inspector did not move; his little eyes still maintained their careful watch on the young man's face.

"Only you see, you do not happen to be master of this house at present, Mr. Daventry."

"What do you mean? I stand in my aunt's place," John Daventry blustered. "What do you mean, sir?"

"I mean that until Lady Anne's lease of this house expires or is disposed of, her legal heir and representative is her executor and brother, the Rev. and Hon. Augustus Fyvert, rector of North Coton, to whom I have wired, and who will be here by the next train," the inspector said coldly.

CHAPTER VII

"AND NOW," observed the inspector. "I think we will have another look at the sitting-room. There are certain papers that must be gone through."

It was the day after Lady Anne Daventry's death. The inquest had been opened in the morning, but only formal evidence had been taken and, after hearing Dr. Spencer, the coroner had adjourned for a week to give the police time for their inquiries.

Both the inspector and Cardyn had been up most of the night, though so far their efforts had produced no result. The rector of North Coton and his wife had arrived the night before and had been too much overcome by the shock and the horror of Lady Anne's death to be of any assistance. Mr. Fyvert had, however, commissioned Cardyn to stay in the house to investigate the circumstances of Lady Anne's death, in conjunction with the police. John Daventry still remained fuming at his enforced detention, but neither he nor the two girls had attended the inquest.

Bruce Cardyn and the inspector walked back to the house together from the little hall in the side street where the inquest had been held.

Soames himself opened the door for them. His mistress's death was making an old man of him. His usually bland, benevolent-looking face was puckered and miserable; evidently he had been crying; his eyes were red-rimmed and his mouth was twitching.

"Oh, couldn't you have stopped it, Mr. Furnival? All those common men tramping up the stairs and right into my lady's room! To say nothing of seeing my poor lady herself. It is what her ladyship would have hated above everything."

"Her ladyship would have wished her murderer found, Mr. Soames," the inspector said, laying his hand on the man's bowed shoulder. "We have good reason to know that."

"Have you?" Soames gulped down a lump in his throat. "There's one thing I wondered whether I ought to mention to you. It is only a trifle, but—"

"Nothing is a trifle in a case of this kind," the inspector said gravely. "A straw shows which way the wind blows."

"Just so. That is what thought. Otherwise I shouldn't have troubled you—but if you will come this way—"

He went to a small window at the end of the hall, looking into the garden.

"That window is always kept locked, by her ladyship's orders, she being nervous of tramps and so many of them about nowadays. Well, when I went round, as my custom is, to see to the fastenings of the windows and doors, that window was open, at least I should say not fastened, and not quite shut at the top, as if some one had got out hurriedly and not been able to push it up from the outside. I—I'm ashamed to say that I did not regard it of any importance last night—I—we were all so upset about my lady. But, when I heard Mr. Fyvert say this morning that her ladyship must have been stabbed by one of the people in the room, it did strike me that the—the murderer might have been in hiding in the house and rushed in and—and accomplished his purpose while we were all engaged with the man at the window, and then made his escape."

The inspector was looking at the window.

"Very well thought out," he said approvingly. "You would make a first-rate detective. But, if the window were pushed up from the outside as you suggest, there ought to be very distinct footmarks in the flower border below."

"Yes, I suppose there ought," Soames said uncertainly. "But it didn't strike me to look, me being fresh to this kind of thing, as you may say," his voice dying away apologetically.

The inspector threw up the sash, noticing how stiffly it moved as he did so. He leaned out and looked down.

"I believe there are some marks," he said as he withdrew his head. "Mr. Cardyn, suppose we take a look at them from the outside."

He drew the window down again and turned off to the door at the end of the hall, which Soames opened for him. He did not go any farther with the detectives but stood watching them with interest.

The inspector took out a measuring tape and a magnifying-glass. Then he carefully picked out a couple of large flat stones from the rockery and put them on the border so that he could cross it without putting his feet on the mould.

"Four very distinct footmarks," he called out to Cardyn. "Two with their toes turned to the house, as if the man had just let himself down from the window—rather deep, too, as if he had shut it as he stood—and two with their toes turned to the garden as if he had gone off that way. Well, so far so good. We must have impressions made of those footmarks, Mr. Cardyn."

Cardyn did not speak for a moment; his grey eyes were thoughtful as he scrutinized the flower border.

"I see the marks by the window plainly enough. But did the beggar get away? He couldn't have taken a flying leap from where he stood to the gravel path, and yet there are no more footmarks on the flower border."

The inspector smiled grimly.

"Another problem for you, Mr. Cardyn. But what I am wondering is, who made those footmarks?"

Bruce looked surprised.

"Well, of course—" he said.

The inspector went on without noticing any interruption.

"Because I examined all the doors and windows last night an hour before Soames did, and—the window was closed and locked then."

"But what can that mean?" Bruce said slowly.

"Some one has a motive for trying to make us think the murderer was an outsider, and that he escaped that way," the inspector said dryly. "But it is possible to be a little too clever, you know, Mr. Cardyn. Now, think we will station a man over there—by the cedar. He can keep an eye on the footmarks without being seen in return."

They went back to the same door. Soames was hovering about in the hall. He looked at them inquiringly.

"As good impressions as we could hope to get," the inspector said patronizingly. "We shall lay the fellow by the heels very soon now."

"I am glad to hear that—for her poor ladyship's sake." The man blew his nose noisily and turned away. "You see it is very upsetting, to them that knew my lady well. And me having been in the family, boy and man, between thirty and forty years."

"Ay! It will come hard on you old ones— like losing one of your own," the inspector said sympathetically. "Between thirty and forty years, you say?"

"Thirty-eight years it will be next Martinmas. The Squire's first wife was alive then, and her daughter, pretty Miss Marjory."

"Mrs. Balmaine, you mean?" the inspector questioned with a sudden accession of interest. "Was she like her daughter?"

"Not much." Soames blew his nose again. "She was darker than Miss Margaret Balmaine, and taller, but she was the apple of her father's eye. He was never the same after she went away. He was proud of Mr. Christopher and Mr. Frank, but they never came up to Miss Marjorie with him."

"I wonder he didn't forgive her marriage, then," Cardyn remarked.

"He would, if she had ever asked him. It was her never troubling about him again that broke her father's heart. And then she died."

"Ah, well! We all have to come to it, Mr. Soames." The inspector gave him a farewell nod. "Now, Mr. Cardyn, we have our work cut out for to-day."

Bruce Cardyn gave himself a mental shake.

For the time being he seemed lost in a sort of dream. His thoughts were very far away as he followed the inspector to Lady Anne's sitting-room.

Nothing could have looked less like the scene of a tragedy. There was nothing to show what had happened. By Inspector Furnival's orders everything had been left exactly as it was at the time of the death, except that what remained of Lady Anne herself had been carried across to her bedroom. The teacups and saucers they had been using stood where the members of Lady Anne's last tea-party had hurriedly set them down when the alarm was raised. The very hot cakes that Soames had dropped when he caught sight of the face at the window still lay on the floor. Some of them had been trodden into Lady Anne's beautiful carpet. The silver cover had rolled or been kicked under the table; the dish itself, with one cake still on it, was near the escritoire.

The inspector's grey eyes looked round appraisingly.

"Now, once more, show me where you all sat, Mr. Cardyn."

Bruce pointed out Dorothy Fyvert's place at the tea-table, his own chair in close proximity, John Daventry's and Margaret Balmaine's near Lady Anne's.

On the flap of the escritoire the little bits of jewellery lay in their open cases, Lady Anne's teacup beside them. On the floor beneath was a deep stain, a silent witness to the tragedy. Inspector Furnival, stepping gingerly among the cakes, went over to the window farthest from the escritoire, which was wide open as it had been left the day before.

He stretched himself out and twisted himself round, staring up and down and both sides.

"I'm afraid your man was not much of a shadower, Mr. Cardyn. In the summer-house, you say he was stationed? I should have said it was impossible for anybody, or anything, to get at this window without being seen."

"So should I," Cardyn acknowledged. "Yet Brooks is one of our most careful men. He allows, though, that he was watching the terrace below, more than the actual window itself. He swears that no one either climbed up from the terrace or came down again."

The inspector took another look.

"He might have put a ladder up possibly without leaving any trace, but he certainly did not climb up by the creeper, that I swear. There isn't not a twig broken as far down as can see. I'll have a look at the roof later on. But now this escritoire. We will just glance through the contents, and then seal it up. Lady Anne kept a diary—I think we will take it away to examine it."

Most of the drawers in the escritoire were unlocked, many of them stood open, as they had been: left when Lady Anne was searching for any trace of the missing jewels. But so far as casual glance could see there was nothing in them that bore upon the present case. Right at the back of the secret cavity, where the pearls had been kept, the inspector's keen eyes had noticed some papers, not rolled up or fastened together in a packet, but looking as though they had been hastily thrust in at odd moments.

He pulled them out; some of them had superscriptions written across the envelopes. "From my son Christopher"; "From my boy Frankie"; two or three older far—"From my husband."

The inspector laid all these reverently aside after a cursory glance. Then he took up the handful of odd ones that remained. Some of them were quite recent. He opened the first.

"'From your loving niece, Dorothy Fyvert,'" he read. "Now why did the old lady preserve this, wonder?"

"She was very fond of Miss Fyvert," Bruce said quickly.

"Yes," the inspector assented dryly. "This is the letter, Mr. Cardyn. It is dated from Barminster Court: 'Dearest Aunt Anne, I am in dreadful trouble. There is no one—no one to whom I can turn but you. I want five hundred pounds at once. You have often talked of leaving me money. Will you give it me now instead? If you will, I will thank you and bless your name for ever. Oh, dear Aunt Anne, my need is dire as you would realize if I could explain to you. Help me for mercy's sake.'"

Across the sheet there was scrawled, in the shaky handwriting that had become very familiar to Bruce Cardyn since his coming to Charlton Crescent, the one word "Refused."

The inspector handed it to Cardyn with a keen glance at the young man's averted face.

"Miss Fyvert would not have murdered her aunt for five times five hundred pounds. Faugh! The very idea is unthinkable. Besides"—growing calmer—"we have no proof that Lady Anne's death would give Miss Fyvert the five hundred pounds she wanted."

"I feel sure that Miss Fyvert comes into a considerable amount of money on her own account," the inspector said gravely. "But at any rate Miss Fyvert is supposed to be engaged to Mr. John Daventry, who certainly succeeds to much of Lady Anne's wealth automatically—I mean under her late husband's will. Still, I don't know. I wonder whether she got her five hundred, and how, but we shall have to hear her explanation."

"I should say there was a much greater motive for John Daventry to commit the murder than for a girl who might and might not marry him," Bruce said sarcastically. "There is many a slip between the cup and the lip, you know."

"Undoubtedly there is," the inspector agreed. "Still, I think we will have a little confidential talk with Miss Dorothy Fyvert." He was thrusting the rest of the papers back into their hiding-place as he spoke. "These all date farther back." Bruce Cardyn went over to the window. He was anxious above all things that the inspector should not guess the secret he had hitherto guarded so carefully, and, ostrich-like, fancied the Ferret's keen eyes had not even suspected. As he stood there looking up and down it was impossible that the memory of yesterday's tragedy, of the ghastly face at the window, should not recur to his mind. Was the form that had looked so shadowy that of a living man or woman, or was it some visitant from another world? Plain matter-of-fact man as Cardyn had hitherto considered himself, he could not answer the question. As he leaned out still farther, a tiny fluttering thread of white caught his eyes. It was in the ivy, just below the window ledge. He stretched down his arm and picked it out. Then he laid it on the palm of his hand and gazed at it curiously. It looked like a thread torn from a piece of muslin, and he remembered the shadowy veil that had seemed to float round that white face. He was just about to show it to the inspector, when he was startled by a sharp exclamation from the other.

"The diary!"

Cardyn turned quickly.

"Lady Anne Daventry's diary," Inspector Furnival repeated. "It is gone."

"Gone!" Bruce Cardyn stepped back. "What do you mean? I saw it on the writing-flap when we came here after the body was moved—a square book bound in grey leather with 'Diary' written in gold across it and a tiny gold lock which was locked."

"It was here then of course," the inspector said. "I noticed it particularly, for I was in two minds whether I should begin to read it last night, but there was so much to be done that I decided to leave it until after the inquest to-day. Now, dolt, ass that am, I shall never forgive myself, some one has been before me."

"But who could have taken it?" Cardyn looked as amazed as he felt. "And how could anyone get into the room at all? You had the key."

"It has not been out of my possession for a moment," the inspector said. "But that book held a secret that might have hanged some one—and that some one had the means of getting into the room."

Cardyn's eyes turned to the open window.

"Suppose—suppose the—the man came back?" he hazarded.

"And got into the room and got out again without being seen by the two men watching—I think not," the inspector observed.

Then, while the two men were still staring at one another, there came an oddly incongruous sound in the stillness—the sharp ring of the telephone bell.

There was a moment's hesitation, then the inspector took up the receiver.

"Hullo! Furnival speaking. Who are you?"

"Wilkins, Scotland Yard," came back the answer. "The pearls—the long string with the diamond clasp for which we were to make inquiries—they were found at the first place we went to."

"Where was that?"

"Messrs. Spagnum and Thirgood, Bond Street. Sold there last month by Lady Anne Daventry herself."

CHAPTER VIII

"IT IS, take it all in all, about the queerest case I was ever engaged upon."

Inspector Furnival was the speaker. He and Bruce Cardyn were in a taxi on their way to Messrs. Spagnum and Thirgood's. Furnival was keeping Cardyn religiously by his side during his investigations—a fact that was beginning to puzzle the younger detective, with whom it was more or less a tradition that the "Force" distrusted all private or unofficial detectives.

"I expect we shall find that they have made a mistake at Spagnum and Thirgood's," Bruce rejoined. "Probably the thief said they were sent by Lady Anne Daventry."

"Likely enough," the detective assented, his small eyes looking particularly alert as their taxi stopped before a well known jeweller's establishment in Bond Street.

Inspector Furnival and his companion, on the production of the former's card, were shown at once to the manager's office. That functionary received them affably.

"I have been expecting you, gentlemen," he said at once. "Come about this matter of Lady Anne Daventry's pearls, haven't you? What a terrible affair this murder of hers is! You might have knocked me down with a feather when I saw it in this morning's paper. Lady Anne Daventry was such an old customer of ours. I feel as if it were a personal loss. Was the crime committed to obtain money, inspector?"

The inspector graciously admitted that it might have been, and asked to see the pearls.

The manager produced them from a safe close by.

"I thought you would want to see them first thing. Here they are. You see there is no mistake about them."

The inspector took the much talked-of pearls in his hand and examined them. They had all been matched with great care both in size and colour, and the clasp was unmistakable.

Inspector Furnival drew a deep breath.

"Yes. It is the pearls right enough. Now, who brought them to you?"

"Lady Anne Daventry herself," the manager answered promptly. "She came about them twice."

"Lady Anne Daventry herself!"

For once the inspector was really amazed.

"Who told you it was Lady Anne Daventry?"

"Who told me it was Lady Anne Daventry?" the manager repeated explosively. "Why, bless my life, inspector, don't you understand that I know Lady Anne Daventry personally? I have only been manager here the last six months. Before then I was head assistant for some twenty years. I have seen Lady Anne here on many occasions, and since she grew more invalided I have waited on her at the house in Charlton Crescent on several occasions with trays of jewellery from which she would select a wedding or birthday present. It was a great pleasure to me to know that she was well enough to come here again."

The inspector regarded him keenly.

"Do you seriously mean to tell me that you really believe it was Lady Anne Daventry herself who brought the pearls here?"

It was the manager's turn to look amazed now.

"I tell you that I know it was Lady Anne Daventry. Her first visit was preceded by a note saying that she was coming, so we were expecting her."

"Was the note written by Lady Anne herself?" questioned the inspector sharply.

The manager hesitated.

"N—o; I don't think it was. It was written on her paper I know, for I remember noticing her crest, but it was written, I presume, by her secretary."

"Have you the letter?"

The manager shook his head.

"I should say it is not in the least likely. If you wish I will have inquiries made. But it was not regarded as of any importance, especially after Lady Anne's visit."

"It is most important that it should be found now, though."

The manager shrugged his shoulders as he said a few words down a speaking tube. It was evident to Bruce Cardyn, watching him, that he looked upon the inspector as both interfering and officious.

"Now with regard to the price?" the inspector went on. "What did you give her for them? And in what form? There is no record of such a transaction in her bank book."

"No," the manager paused. "Of course in an ordinary case all details would be confidential. But I have no choice here."

"None!" the inspector interposed firmly.

"We offered two thousand for it," the manager said reluctantly, "and she accepted at once. As to the form, she explained that she did not wish anyone to know that she had parted with her pearls. We gathered that she wanted the money for some member of her family who had got into trouble, therefore she did not want to have a cheque as it would be easily traced. She asked us to give her the amount in notes. We gave her that day ten notes of a hundred each and arranged to pay the other instalment at a later date. We should, of course, have sent it to her, but she explained that she would come for it in person, as practically all her correspondence passed through her secretary's hands."

"Then this second thousand—"

"It is still waiting for her. Some three days ago we received a note from her saying that she would come to our establishment to complete her business with us on Thursday, the 5th of February, which, of course, is next week. We replied that everything would be ready for her. The next thing we saw was in the paper telling of her cruel murder. You can hardly imagine what a shock it gave us."

"It must have done," the inspector agreed, a certain amount of sympathy in his tone. "And now, I am afraid you must prepare for another shock. Lady Anne Daventry did not sell her pearls to you. She had not found out that they were missing until the afternoon of her death when she wanted to show them to some friends. She herself summoned Scotland Yard to her assistance and I was on the point of starting for Charlton Crescent to interview her on the subject when the news of her brutal murder arrived."

"What!" The manager was staring at the inspector as though he doubted the evidence of his own ears. "But I tell you it was Lady Anne who—"

"I am afraid you have been deceived by a clever impostor," the inspector said gravely. "The person who sold you the pearls was not Lady Anne Daventry herself, but some one impersonating her."

"But it is impossible," stuttered the manager. "I tell you knew Lady Anne not only by sight, but had often spoken to her. I am certain it was Lady Anne who brought the pearls."

"Well, if you are right, the mystery only deepens," the inspector said diplomatically. "Will you please tell us all about the interview. Every detail of it, so far as you remember."

The manager waited a moment.

"It—there is so little to say," he began at last. "Lady Anne arrived punctually at the time she had fixed on the Friday of last week. I went out to receive her and with her man on the other side helped her from the carriage. From there she walked in here with my arm and the stick on the other side. Her man carried the case containing the pearls. I may say that Lady Anne explained that she would have brought her maid with her, but that she did not wish the woman, who I understood had been with her for many years, to know that she had parted with her pearls. The interview was very quickly over. We had valued Lady Anne's pearls for her some years before, so that she knew what to expect and we were quite satisfied to give the price she asked. I helped her back to her carriage, and she drove off promising, as I say, to call to complete the transaction next week, on the 5th of February."

"I wonder why she did not arrange to come sooner," the inspector said, speaking as if half to himself, while his small grey eyes watched every change in the other's face from beneath their lowered lids.

The manager spread out his hands.

"Who can account for the vagaries of these great ladies? Lady Anne did, however, say something about having something else to bring us to-day."

"And you really noticed nothing unaccustomed or strange in her voice or manner?"

"Nothing!" the manager said decidedly. "She talked in her usual brisk and rather snappy manner—for there is no denying she was a snappy old lady, you know, inspector! And she wore the same sort of clothes she always did—a rather full mantle, some magnificent furs and a regular Victorian bonnet. No, I noticed nothing particular about her except—But, no, there couldn't be anything in that."

"Perhaps you will let us have it?" suggested the inspector. "We can't afford to neglect any clue, however slight."

"Well, it was nothing of course," the manager went on. "But I noticed that she signed the receipt without removing her gloves. I remarked it because I remembered the big diamond she generally wore and glanced to see if it was still there. I thought it a little strange perhaps that she did not take off her glove, but of course one can understand that crippled with rheumatism as she was it may have been very painful to pull her gloves off and on."

"H'm!" the inspector scratched the side of his nose reflectively, with the handle of his fountain pen. "May I see the receipt?"

"Certainly!" The manager unlocked his desk. "Here it is. Only the signature is in Lady Anne's writing of course."

"Of course," assented the inspector. "Mr. Cardyn, what do you make of this? Is it Lady Anne's writing? This gentleman was Lady's Anne's private secretary," he added as Bruce bent over the paper.

Undoubtedly it was almost identical with the crabbed and shaking handwriting that had become very familiar to Bruce Cardyn of late. Almost—and yet, was it quite? Bruce could not answer the question to his own satisfaction. At last he looked up.

"If it is not Lady Anne Daventry's signature it is a remarkably clever imitation. But—I am not sure—"

The inspector handed the receipt back to the manager.

"Take care of it, sir. We may want it later. And—one more question, and then I will not detain you longer. Did Lady Anne come in her own carriage?"

"I really couldn't be certain," the manager said, beginning to look uneasy. "It was a private car and there were two men on the box, so I took it for granted it was her own, but I can't say any more."

"Well, I am very grateful to you for allowing us to take up so much of your valuable time," the inspector said, getting up. "And they say gratitude is a sense of favours to come—I am afraid we shall take up more of it yet. Good morning."

When they were out of sight of Messrs. Spagnum and Thirgood's, and their taxi was bowling as swiftly as the traffic would allow towards Bayswater Road, Bruce Cardyn looked at the inspector.

"Did it strike you that manager fellow looked a trifle pale at the end?"

"Afraid of losing his job if he let himself be taken in by an impostor, however clever, I expect," the inspector explained blandly. "But"—throwing himself round and almost facing the young man—"this is a queer case, as queer a case as ever I came across. As a rule one is bothered to find a clue—here the clues seem to tumble out under one's nose all the time. The difficulty is they all lead in different directions, and I'm blessed if I can make out the right one as yet. Now—"

He stopped and looked out at the traffic without speaking.

"Now—?" Bruce Cardyn repeated curiously.

The inspector gave an odd little laugh.

"I am wondering whether Lady Anne Daventry did not sell her jewels herself and simply wanted us to imagine that they were stolen. Such a case is not without a parallel in the annals of the British aristocracy."

"I am quite sure there was nothing of that kind about the loss of Lady Anne's jewels," Bruce Cardyn said firmly. "Besides, surely her murder shows—"

"So you imagine Lady Anne was murdered by the person who stole the pearls?" The inspector questioned, fixing the young man with his gimletlike gaze. "And why?"

Bruce Cardyn felt as if the solid ground was melting away beneath his feet.

"So that the identity of the thief should not be discovered," he said slowly.

"So that is your theory," said the inspector with another of those queer little laughs. "But does it not strike you as odd, Mr. Cardyn, that, if the pearl thief were also the murderer, Lady Anne should have been killed just a week before the day fixed for the payment of the second half of the purchase money, and what about the secret poisoning? Ah, ah, Mr. Cardyn, is it possible that you private inquiry gentlemen still have something to learn from the real article?"

CHAPTER IX

IT WAS A WEEK to the day since the murder of Lady Anne Daventry.

Inspector Furnival was sitting in the library on the first floor, ostensibly looking over the notes in his pocket-book, with an occasional glance at the pile of the daily papers that lay on the table beside him, in reality keeping a keen watch on the door leading into the hall which he had left open.

Lady Anne's funeral had taken place the previous day. Her will had directed that she should be buried in the nearest place of interment to the place in which she died, "having," as that document stated, "an objection to having my body cart- ed about the country." So that instead of a stately funeral at Daventry there had been a very simple affair in a big London cemetery. The time of the service had been kept secret or there would have been the usual crowd of sightseers. But there was scarcely anyone about when Lady Anne's coffin with its plain black handles, as directed in her will, was borne over the short grass to its last resting- place. John Daventry and the rector of North Coton had been the chief mourners and then there had been other Fyverts and Daventrys—conspicuous among them the present Lord Fyvert—the dead lady's nephew. Bruce Cardyn walked with the inspector and behind them came the servants, Soames and Pirnie at the head of them. The service had been as brief as possible, and most of the mourners had dispersed without returning to Charlton Crescent.

The adjourned inquest was to be opened to-day at eleven o'clock. It was now nine, and the inspector who was an inde- fatigably early riser had been up for hours, and having break- fasted was now at liberty to read the papers, and to carry out a private plot of his own before going on to the inquiry.

Lady Anne Daventry's murder had captured the public im- agination in no ordinary degree. The rank and age of the vic- tim, the mystery surrounding the crime and the fact that the newspapers just now had nothing particular on hand had com- bined to make the Charlton Crescent Mystery, as it was called, the principal topic of interest.

The inspector ran through the papers quickly. As he had expected, such headings as "Charlton Crescent Murder." "Re- ported Clue." "Who was the man at the window?" were con- spicuous on the first page. But surprises for Inspector Furnival were hardly likely to come in the daily press. He soon turned back to his notes, and was knitting his brows together over some knotty problem when Soames came into the room. The man was looking white and shaken.

"I have been told, Mr. Furnival, that I shall be one of the first witnesses called to-day, because I was the first to see the man at the window."

"Quite likely!" the inspector assented. "But it will only be a matter of form, you know, Mr. Soames. You will not find it at all alarming. Just say what you saw. That is all."

"Thank you. But I have never come in contact with anything of the kind before, and can't say I like the prospect of speaking right out in court."

"Oh, well, it will soon be over," the inspector said genially. "You look cold. Stir the fire. I didn't notice how hollow it was burning. But, there, I forgot. Don't you high-class flunkeys get a footman to poke the fire for you?"

Soames gave a sickly smile as he paused, poker in hand.

"Oh, we are not all quite so bad as they make us out. My poor lady would have told you that I always liked to do everything in her room myself."

"Ah, well, I am glad that her ladyship recognized your long years of devoted service," the inspector went on.

Soames stirred the hot coals into a brisk flame.

"Yes, Mr. Furnival, her ladyship has left all us head servants, if we were with her at the time of her death, five hundred pounds each. That is, me and Miss Pirnie, and the chauffeur that used to be the coachman, and the head gardener—we all came with her from the Keep. The other ones have smaller sums according to their time of service."

The inspector nodded. No one was better acquainted with the terms of the will than he.

"You were here when—" he was beginning when his quick ear caught the sound of a "click" in the hall. He got up leisurely.

"Somebody at the telephone—I will just explain—"

Soames would have stepped forward to open the door already standing ajar, but the inspector waved him aside and went into the hall.

"Ah, Miss Fyvert," he said suavely. "I see you did not know the extensions had been cut off. The only phone left now is this one in the library."

Dorothy Fyvert stared at him, receiver in hand.

"Who has done this? How stupid and inconvenient!" with an evident effort to speak naturally.

"Well, I am afraid I must plead guilty to having given the order. Detectives have to do all sorts of odd things, you know, Miss Fyvert. But I am very sorry if it has inconvenienced you," the inspector went on politely. "Will you not come in to the library?"

"Well, I want to send a message to the dressmaker," Dorothy hesitated. "It was rather important, but—"

"Shall I see if the line is clear for you?" the inspector inquired blandly as he held open the library door.

Miss Fyvert hesitated. She was not looking well to-day, as the inspector had noticed at once. Her face was very white; all her pretty colour had faded; her eyes had deep blue half-circles under them, and the eyes themselves glanced about nervously. She bit her lip now.

"No, thank you! After all I do not know that I will ring up Madame Benoit. I do not know that there is any real need."

"Oh, but I have always been told that a lady's appointment with her dressmaker was most important," the inspector said. "Madame Benoit, you said." He paused with the receiver in his hand. "The address, please."

Miss Fyvert paused a minute, but the inspector's gimlet-like eyes were filed upon her.

"17 Clonnell Street, off Wigmore Street," she said with a little laugh. "Really, inspector, you are a very determined man. I don't wonder the criminal classes are afraid of you."

"I hope they are," the inspector said grimly. "Here. Why, we have been lucky enough to get on at once. Now, Miss Fyvert."

He handed her the receiver and waited while she gave her few directions about a dress that did not fit, and made an appointment for some alterations. Then she put down the receiver with a hand that visibly trembled.

"Thank you very much, Inspector Furnival. If I had known your telephone arrangements I would not have disturbed you."

The inspector smiled faintly.

"It has been no trouble, Miss Fyvert. I am glad I happened to be here," he said truthfully. "I have been looking for an opportunity of having a few words with you. Perhaps you could spare me a few minutes now?"

The girl's white face turned scarlet, slowly, painfully.

"I do not think I can stay this morning," she faltered. "I have to go to this terrible inquest and then my little sister is not well. I am very anxious about her. I cannot think what is the matter with her."

"I am sorry to hear that." The inspector placed a chair for her and something about his gaze compelled her to take it. "But children are often up and down. I have six at home so ought to know. As for the inquest, I am anxious to have a few words with you before that."

"The—the inquest?" Dorothy faltered. "But that is this morning. I really do not see—"

"Oh, there will be plenty of time before the inquest," the inspector said easily. He had placed her chair so that she faced the window, and now he stood opposite so that he, though in the shadow himself, got the light full upon her. "There is sure to be a crowd there—at the inquest, I mean—and it would not be wondered at if a young lady like yourself lost her head a little. So I thought if you and I had a talk first it might make things easier for you."

"But I can't tell them anything!" the girl exclaimed wildly, clasping her hands closely together. "I was in the room when Aunt Anne was—when she died, but I did not see anything. I could not tell them anything."

The inspector coughed.

"In a case like this, we have to look at the matter all round. And first and foremost there is the question of motive. There were five people in the room—"

"Five people!" Dorothy interrupted him. "Six, you mean, for you surely cannot omit the man at the window?"

The inspector accepted the correction.

"Six, then. Of course you saw this sixth—the man at the window—yourself, Miss Fyvert?"

"Well, I can't say exactly," Dorothy said honestly. "I was at the tea-table, and was so amazed to see Soames drop the cakes that I was looking at him, and only had the most casual glance at something moving at the window. Also, of course, everybody made a rush for the window, so that they got between."

"And you saw and heard nothing else?" the inspector said sharply.

"Well, I have told myself since that it must have been a mistake," Dorothy said doubtfully. "But I did fancy at the time that I heard a soft eerie laugh."

"Ah! You did?" the inspector's eyes grew keen. "Now where did it seem to come from, up or down, or one side?"

"Really, I couldn't tell," Dorothy said, a strange look compounded of fear and some subtler emotion coming over her face. "It just seemed to be in the air. I can't tell you any more, Mr. Furnival."

"Ah—um—well!" The inspector dismissed the subject. "Well, you went with the others to the window, I presume!" he proceeded.

"I went with them," she acquiesced. "I think I was the last to reach the window. I remember Soames standing aside for me. And then it was all confusion till we heard that horrible groan and cry and I found out that poor Aunt Anne had been stabbed."

"The last to reach the window," mused the inspector. "H'm! Now, Miss Fyvert, can you tell me of any one of the others who was near you all the time right up to the moment when you heard that groan?"

Dorothy drew her delicate brows together, her blue eyes looked puzzled and worried. "I don't know. I don't think so," she said slowly at last. "It seems to me that Mr. John Daventry was close to me a good deal of the time, but could not swear to the exact moment when we heard the groan."

"I see. I wish you could," the inspector said. "Now with regard to this question of motive, it is a curious thing that every person in the room would be better off at Lady Anne's death. To you she bequeathed her pearls and her jewels."

"Some of her other jewels," Dorothy corrected. "Both my little sister and Miss Balmaine have legacies; Mr. Daventry also. But, Mr. Furnival" —her blue eyes growing wide with horror, her voice vibrating with indignation—"you cannot mean to suggest that I killed Aunt Anne in order to obtain her legacy. I did not even know that she had left the pearls to me. You cannot think—"

"I do not think—I do not suggest—anything," the inspector interrupted gravely. "It is my duty to deal with facts as they are. Now, Miss Fyvert, I happen to know that a very short time ago you were in urgent need of a large sum of money. You wrote to Lady Anne and asked her to help you; and she refused—"

"How in the world do you know that?" Dorothy gasped, every vestige of colour fading from her cheeks, even her lips turning blue, the pupils of her eyes distending until the eyes themselves looked black.

For answer the inspector held her letter to Lady Anne out to her.

"Your handwriting, I think?"

The girl bent her head. She was biting her underlip, her fingers were turning and intertwining themselves together.

"Miss Fyvert," the inspector went on, a kindlier note creeping into his voice as he noticed the girl's agitation, "there is a saying that a man should have no secrets from his doctor or his lawyer. Believe me, in a case of this kind it is best to have no secrets from the police. Now will you tell me whether you obtained that money and how?"

"I—I can't," faltered the girl. "I do not think"—rallying all her courage—"that you have any right to ask me. You see that Aunt Anne refused me. The rest cannot concern you."

"Everything concerns me that may bear upon the doings of any of you in the room that evening. Won't you be frank with me, Miss Fyvert? A few words to me now may save you much unpleasantness later on. In a court of law you can be compelled to answer."

"Nobody can compel me," the girl said, raising her head proudly. "Besides, are not people who are accused warned not to speak because what they say may be used in evidence against them."

"But you are not accused!" the inspector said quietly. "No one is accused yet. I said that any one of you four—Mr. Daventry, Miss Balmaine, yourself and Soames, the butler—might be accused, because you were known to be in the room."

"No!" Dorothy contradicted in a defiant tone. "Once more you have forgotten the man at the window—the Cat Burglar as they call him in the papers—and—and Mr. Cardyn."

The softening in her tone did not escape the inspector's quick hearing.

"Ah! the Cat Burglar!" he repeated, an odd little inflection in his voice. "Well, I do not see how the Cat Burglar outside can have much to do with the murder of Lady Anne Daventry from the inside. As for Mr. Cardyn, I think we must put him out of court, because—I am speaking to you confidentially now, Miss Fyvert—he is a private detective engaged by Lady Anne herself, to prevent this very thing that happened—"

"What! Mr. Cardyn a detective! I do not believe it!" Dorothy caught her breath sharply. "I am certain he is not—could not be anything of the kind."

The inspector raised his eyebrows. "I assure you he is. But now, Miss Fyvert, I tell you what I am going to do. I'm going to leave you here alone for a few minutes just to think things over before we start for the inquest. I think, on reflection, you will see that it is best to tell me everything."

"I shall not, I will not," Dorothy contradicted hotly.

The inspector paid no heed. He left the room with his usual catlike tread and Dorothy was alone.

Her first proceeding was to jump up and take a few steps up and down the room, her breath coming in quick strong gasps, her small brown hands gripping one another.

"I do not believe it—I know it is not true," she said passionately to herself.

Then she threw herself back in her chair, her breast panting, her foot tapping the floor.

"What am I to do?" she cried to herself. "Heaven help me, I do not know what to do now."

At this moment Bruce Cardyn opened the door and looked in.

"You sent for me, inspector? Miss Fyvert" —his tone changing to one of consternation—"you are in trouble. Can I help you?"

Wrath dried Dorothy's tears. She dropped the handkerchief.

"You! No! You would only make things worse for me. I have been told—"

"What have you been told?" Bruce stood before her, his arms folded. Instinct told him what was coming.

"You know!" the girl said scornfully. "I have been told—the—the inspector has told me—you are here to watch, to pry—Oh, it is loathsome—loathsome! I wonder that a man can stoop so low!"

Bruce Cardyn took rapid counsel with himself. The inspector must have had some motive for giving away the secret he had hitherto guarded so successfully.

"You have heard that I am a detective," he said quietly. "Does that seem so terrible a thing to you?"

Dorothy struck her hands together passionately.

"It seems horrible, detestable! To spend your time trying to find out other people's secrets—to be a spy, an informer! Would it be possible for a man to sink lower? And that it should be you—you who have done this vile thing!"

The hot blood flew to Cardyn's brow. For a moment he struggled to find words to answer. At last he said, controlling his voice:

"Does it seem so dreadful a thing to you to put oneself on the side of the law? The innocent— the innocent have nothing to fear from a detective, Miss Fyvert."

"Oh, yes, they have!" Dorothy said wrathfully. "You may be quite innocent, but they will go prying and poking about trying to find out things that are no concern of theirs all the same. And you—you who saved me from that terrible fire—whom I have looked upon as a friend—" Tears choked her utterance.

The anger her words had caused in Bruce Cardyn's heart died down, to be succeeded by pity and a stronger, simpler emotion, that even to himself he had hardly dared yet to acknowledge.

"It has been a great joy—a supreme honour for me that you have allowed me to count myself among your friends," he said quietly. "For the sake of that friendship, will you listen to me for one minute? Your aunt, Lady Anne, sent for me; she told me that she was frightened, that some member of her household was trying to murder her—she did not know who—and she asked me to come here as her secretary and find out which one it could be. It seemed to be then—it seems to me now—a very pitiful case. Here was a woman, old, alone, fearing the death that was lurking near all the time, not knowing from what corner it might come. I promised to do my best for her. Heaven knows I meant to make her safe!"

"But you didn't," Dorothy said scornfully. "You didn't pry about in the right direction, you see, Mr. Cardyn."

"I did not," Bruce Cardyn acknowledged, a faraway look in his grey eyes. "I shall never forgive myself for having failed her, and yet I do not see what could have done—that I did not do. Now—now I have sworn to avenge her murder. When I have fulfilled my vow, I shall come to you and say, I am a detective no longer. Will you give me a word of hope, Miss Fyvert, will you be my friend again?" He made a slight gesture as though to put out his hand.

But Dorothy would not take it. She put both hers firmly behind her.

"I shall say, however much you give it up, the remembrance of what you have done and been in the past will cling to you still," she said cuttingly. "Friends with a detective—a spy! No, thank you, Mr. Cardyn!"

CHAPTER X

THE HALL AT THE BACK of Charlton Crescent where the inquest on Lady Anne Daventry was resumed was crammed to its utmost limit when the inquiry was reopened. Crowds waited outside, unable to get in, but hoping for a glance at those who were to give evidence to-day. The curiosity of the sightseers was not to be gratified this morning, however. A private car with the rector of North Coton, his wife and the two girls came first. They were followed quickly by another car containing Bruce Cardyn, John Daventry, Inspector Furnival and Soames.

They were both driven through the crowd to a back entrance, and while the sightseers were still watching for "the Five" they were safely inside the court-house.

The inquest was held in a big room, while there sat at the table near the coroner the counsels who held watching briefs for the five and for the Fyvert and Daventry families, and, much to the surprise of the general public who did not see the connexion, for Messrs. Spagnum and Thirgood. Close behind them again were the solicitors who instructed them, and the seats allotted to the witnesses. Every other seat, every other inch of standing room was quickly filled when the coroner took his place and the doors were opened.

Francis Herbert Soames was the first witness called and there was a sharp stir of expectation through the court.

Soames looked as urbane and dignified as ever as he made his way through the crowd, but it was evident to a keen observer that the tragic events of the past fortnight had left their mark upon him. His shoulders were more bowed, his face was paler, even his lips were white as he kissed the book.

After the preliminaries were over the coroner bade him tell the story of the afternoon of Lady Anne's death to the jury, as clearly and as concisely as possible.

He stated his length of service in the Daventry family and gave his age as fifty-six, to the surprise of the sightseers, who thought he looked more. Then he passed on to what he saw on the afternoon of the 29th.

"It was getting dark," he began, "and I took up another relay of hot cakes to my lady's sitting-room, knowing how fond the young ladies were of them. I had got in the room and was surprised to find how dark it was, it not being my lady's custom to sit in the gloaming. One of the young ladies began to joke about the cakes," he went on, a huskiness coming in his voice for the first time. "I was just opposite the window, and as I answered Miss Dorothy something seemed to move across the glass. I looked more closely and saw a white face—a noticeably white face, staring in at us. I was so startled, sir," looking apologetically at the coroner, "that I am ashamed to say I dropped the plate of cakes in my hand and called out. I often say to myself that if I hadn't done so my poor lady might have been alive now. For there was such an outcry when Mr. Daventry and the young ladies saw the face at the window that the murderer was able to come in and work his wicked will on my lady. The next thing I heard, while we were all looking out, was that dreadful gasping cry, and when we turned round, there was my lady choking her life-blood away, with that dagger sticking out of her breast."

He stopped. The coroner looked at his notes.

"You say, 'the murderer was able to come in.' Why do you say he came in? Did you see him? Did you hear any movement?"

"No, sir, no." The witness paused as if to suppress some emotion. "But it stands to reason that some one did come in. It is impossible to suppose—"

"You are not asked to suppose, witness," the coroner interposed. "Did you or did you not hear or see anything to show you that another person had entered the room."

"No, I did not, sir," the witness replied unwillingly.

"Now with regard to this man at the window," the coroner went on, after another glance at his notes, "will you tell us exactly about the state of these windows—this one and the other? Were they open or closed?"

"This one was open a few inches from the top, sir. The one nearest her ladyship—not the one the man came to—was a little open. The other was latched. They were just as my lady always gave orders they should be, sir."

"I have no doubt of that," said the coroner. "Now can you conceive it possible that a man could have got through either of them into the room?"

"Well, I don't know, sir. I couldn't. But then I am not a Cat Burglar."

In spite of the gravity of the case a ripple of laughter ran through the crowd at the idea of the portly and superior butler posing as a cat burglar. When it had been suppressed by the usher, the coroner said:

"One more question, please, Mr. Soames. You speak of the last gasping cry her ladyship gave. Did it sound to you as if your lady were trying to call out, to say some words?"

"Well, no, sir, I can't say that it did!" the witness said doubtfully. "But then you see there was such a commotion and was that upset by seeing the face at the window that I didn't realize what was happening, or how important it was that should be able to remember all that passed."

"I see." The coroner wrote a few lines on his paper. "You can go, now, witness, but you must hold yourself in readiness, for you may be wanted later."

Soames's place in the witness-box was taken by John Daventry, who looked the model of a healthy young Englishman as he stood up to face the crowded court, though his usually good-tempered expression had been replaced by an air of morose defiance. He took the oath and kissed the book and answered the first few formal questions in a surly fashion that turned the sympathies of most men against him. Asked to give his account of the events of that tragic afternoon he responded curtly that it would be just the same as the last witness's, except that he did not see the face at the window till after Soames cried out.

"Nevertheless, put it in your own words, please," the coroner said with an air of calm authority that even John Daventry dared not disregard.

"Well, my aunt had been telling us all about her pearls and showing us her other bits of jewellery and—and—the dagger. And we had been turning them all over and then it was getting dusk and we had tea up. We had so much to talk about that we didn't ring for lights. At last Soames brought us some more hot cakes and dropped them and yelled like mad, and stood pointing at the window. Then I saw some joker looking in—a fellow with an ugly white face. We all ran to the window, but the chap seemed to have got away somehow. And while we were all looking for him there was that cry from Lady Anne and we turned to find her dead or dying with that dagger sticking in her." During this bald recital Daventry's ruddy cheeks had faded almost to the sickly green colour of the evening of the murder. After that first glance at the lookers-on in the well of the court, however, he did not turn that way again, but faced the coroner with shoulders thrown back and squared, and defiant eyes. He seemed in some way to sense the hostile feeling of the waiting crowd.

The coroner held out a plan of the sitting-room to him.

"Will you mark the chair in which you sat, if you please, Mr. Daventry?"

The witness took the plan, scowled at it and finally scored one of the seats with a big black cross.

The coroner scrutinized it. "You were the nearest to the escritoire, to Lady Anne, I see."

"Yes, I was, on that side," John Daventry said gloomily. "But—" a sudden passion springing into his tone—"that doesn't say that I jumped up and stuck a dagger into the poor old lady. Oh, I know what you are driving at, Mr. Coroner! I can see as far through a stone wall as anyone."

"That is a most improper observation to make, Mr. Daventry," the coroner said severely. "Please to confine yourself to the matter in hand. You speak of Lady Anne's last cry—did it sound to you as if she were trying to say something, or only like a cry for help?"

"Well, a bit of both!" John Daventry said sullenly, still smarting under his rebuke. "It was like a gasping choke—and then she tried to say: 'It was—it was—' twice like that, and then she was gone."

"Had you any knowledge of the fact that Lady Anne had some reason to fear that an attempt was likely to be made on her life—had been made unsuccessfully several times in fact?"

John Daventry opened his eyes. "No, I hadn't. And I don't believe it now. The old lady would have been sure to have told me, and I should have taken care to safeguard her."

The coroner coughed. "Not quite so easy as it sounds, perhaps, Mr. Daventry. Now, did this face at the window bear any resemblance to that of anyone you know?"

"Good Lord, no! I should think not!" John Daventry burst out energetically. "A chap with a face like chalk, like a clown's or a mask or something of that sort and a mass of black hair."

There was a pause. The coroner was consulting his notes. At last John Daventry moved as if to leave the box. The coroner stopped him.

"Another question, Mr. Daventry. Is it not a fact that every one in the room benefited by Lady Anne's death?"

"I suppose so," Daventry assented sulkily. "Every one that is to say but the secretary—Cardyn. She didn't leave him anything. He hadn't been there long enough."

"You and Miss Balmaine, I understand, come into a large sum of money between you?"

Daventry nodded. "Yes. Under my uncle's will. He left his large private fortune to his wife for her life, and then to his sons who were killed in the war. Then it was to be divided between me and the heirs of his daughter if any of them were ever discovered. Lady Anne's money went back to her own family, naturally."

It was a long speech for John Daventry, usually one of the most inarticulate of men. At its conclusion he wiped the little beads of perspiration from his brow.

"Now, Mr. Daventry, I understand that you have on several occasions tried to anticipate this reversion," the coroner said, watching him closely.

Daventry stared back at him. "How do you know that? I am not here to answer questions about my private affairs."

"You are here to answer any questions that may throw any light on the death of Lady Anne Daventry," the coroner rejoined severely. "This sort of thing will do you no good, Mr. Daventry. Answer the question, please."

"Well, then, I have," John Daventry said sullenly. "Expenses have gone up and—and the estate doesn't bring in any more. Every fellow flies a few kites nowadays."

"And did this particular kite of yours succeed?" the coroner asked blandly. "Were you able to borrow the money you wanted?"

"No, I wasn't. The blighter wouldn't advance me anything."

The beads of perspiration were plainly visible on Daventry's brow now. Every now and then he dashed his handkerchief across them. "You see, if I died before Lady Anne, they would not have got a penny, it would have gone to Miss Balmaine or failing her to my cousin, Alan Daventry. And Lady Anne was a game old lady—might have lived to be a hundred if it had not been for this scandalous affair. One of the fellows had the cheek to tell me her life was better than mine."

"Quite so!" the coroner said politely. "I think that is all, Mr. Daventry."

John Daventry opened his mouth as if to make some rejoinder, then changed his mind, and, with an awkward bow to the coroner, stepped down from the box and made his way back to his seat next Margaret Balmaine. People looked askance at him as he passed. One or two drew themselves out of his way. There could be no doubt that upon the general public John Daventry had made a most unfavourable impression. He was, as Inspector Furnival had once remarked, the obvious suspect, but the obvious was not always the right.

The inspector's face was inscrutable as ever as he stood up and asked that the inquest might be further adjourned for a fortnight, as the police were making certain inquiries which he hoped by that time might have some definite result.

The coroner shuffled about his papers and consulted the foreman of the jury for a moment. Then, just as he turned to the inspector, one of the jurymen rose.

"Might I put a question to Inspector Furnival on behalf of myself and my colleagues, sir?"

"Oh, certainly," the coroner said at once. "There can be no objection, can there, inspector?"

"Decidedly not, sir." But though the inspector's face was as imperturbable as ever as he turned to face the jury, in his heart he was cursing his interlocutor. None knew better than he how very awkward and inapt these questions of the jurymen often were, of how frequently a criminal had taken fright just at the most critical moment.

"What we want to know is this, sir," the inquisitive juryman persisted. "We have heard a good deal about finger-prints, all of us, one way and another, and we should like to know why Inspector Furnival has not had the handle of the dagger examined for finger-prints, if he has not. And, if he has, why he has not communicated the results of the examination to us."

The suspicion of a smile flitted across the inspector's face. Nothing that was done in all the wonderful artistic and scientific methods of detecting crime employed by the Criminal Investigation Department had so captured the public imagination as this one of finger-prints, he was well aware. Also no one was aware how fallacious such a test might be.

"The usual steps to secure the finger-prints on the dagger handle were taken at once, naturally."

"And the result?" the juror questioned breathlessly.

"We found the finger-prints more or less distinct of all the people in the room, and of Lady Anne Daventry herself."

"No one else? No sixth man?" Another juror burst out.

"Not at this examination. The handle is at present being put under other tests by Sir William Forrester Sanders, the expert. But I may say at once that I do not anticipate any different result."

"Then—the murder must have been committed by one of the five people in the room?"

A shiver of horror passed through his hearers. The witnesses sitting near together in the front of the court drew a little apart and glanced at one another sideways as they waited for the answer.

The inspector bent his head. "So it would seem."

The coroner passed out. The crowd waited, their eyes fixed upon that little group of people in the front. They wanted to see them get up— these five very ordinary-looking men and women, one of whom must be a murderer. Moreover, a murderer of the most cruel and brutal kind, one who had killed a defenceless old woman bound to every one of them by ties of gratitude and duty.

But the ushers began to clear the court. The curious would not be allowed to stare any longer. As they were turning unwillingly to the door, the Five got up. The rector of North Coton with his wife preceded them to the door the courtesy of the coroner had allowed them to use, the two girls came next looking white and frightened in their new mourning. John Daventry and Bruce Cardyn followed, most unwilling companions in adversity. Inspector Furnival brought up the rear, chatting amiably with Soames.

"So it wasn't so very formidable after all, was it?"

"No. Not—not really, of course. They didn't ask me anything about the footsteps under the window at the back of the Hall. I mean those I showed you myself. That puzzled me a bit."

The inspector looked at him with something as like a wink as so dignified a functionary ever permitted himself.

"It doesn't do to tell them everything we know. I may tell you I am following up that clue myself."

Some of the tension died out of the butler's face.

"Then may take it you don't feel sure that it was one of the five in the room that was guilty?"

The inspector gave him a knowing glance.

"I never feel sure of anything in this world. I may tell you in confidence that when I have made those footmarks out I shall have found out who murdered Lady Anne."

"I—I am glad to hear you say that," the man said almost gratefully. "It seemed so dreadful that one of us, one of us who loved her"—he gulped down something in his throat—"should have killed my lady."

When they reached Charlton Crescent again Bruce Cardyn touched the inspector.

"Did you see a tall youngish man, fair, with rather noticeable white teeth, and a monocle fixed in one eye, who sat a little way behind us and apparently took great interest in the case? He was making notes in a book on his knee."

The inspector nodded. "Mr. David Branksome, your predecessor."

"Was he?" For once Cardyn was taken utterly by surprise. "Did you see him apparently pushed close to our party by the jostling of the crowd? In reality he was cleverly edging himself up to Miss Balmaine. I saw him pass something—a note apparently to her."

The inspector laughed a little, and feeling in his waistcoat pocket held out his hand to the younger man. Bruce looked at the grubby piece of paper lying in his palm.

"Mosswolds'—4 o'clock to-morrow."

"An appointment?"

"Looks like it," said the inspector. "We shall have to put in an appearance there, Mr. Cardyn." Bruce glanced at it doubtfully. "But will Miss Balmaine keep the appointment when she finds that she has lost her note?"

"She will not know," the inspector said confidently. "Miss Balmaine like one or two of the others concerned in this remarkable case is just a little too clever, Mr. Cardyn. She managed to read that note, holding it low down in her hand while the people were all round the court. When she had finished she tore it into several pieces and let it fall to the floor, thinking, no doubt, that she was unobserved and that she had done with it for ever. But there was a little ragged boy, who had managed somehow to push himself into the court—a little ragged boy who was close behind her when she dropped it. He picked it up—I am sure it will not surprise you to learn that he is one of my keenest sleuths—he put the pieces together with some bits of stamp paper, took a taxi and was here as soon as we were."

"A smart piece of work altogether!" commented Bruce Cardyn. "'Mosswolds'—a restaurant off Piccadilly, isn't it?"

"Mostyn Street, left off Bond Street," corrected the inspector. "I hear the car is ordered directly after luncheon to-morrow to take the young ladies to the dressmaker's. I expect our young lady will manage to slip away from there. At any rate we shall be ready for her."

"Y—es." Bruce paused and hesitated, then he said slowly, "In spite of the doctor's evidence and also the fact that I know the modern young woman is athletic, I have always doubted the possibility of that blow's having been struck by a woman, inspector."

The inspector looked at him.

"I fancy that an athletic girl of to-day could strike home just as swiftly and just as surely as a man."

"Well, it may be so," Cardyn acknowledged reluctantly. "But I should not call either of the two girls in this case—Miss Fyvert and Miss Balmaine—particularly athletic."

"Miss Fyvert plays hockey and cricket and tennis, takes fencing lessons and rides to hounds. She is no weakling," commented the inspector dryly. "As for Miss Balmaine, she has lived all her life in Australia until the last few months, for the most part at a sheep farm, miles from civilization. That fact speaks for itself."

"Y—es," Bruce acquiesced. "Nevertheless, inspector, I feel quite sure that neither of these girls killed Lady Anne. Miss Fyvert, of course, is out of the question—the idea is so absurd as to be almost farcical. And I do not, in spite of various suspicious happenings, I cannot believe Margaret Balmaine guilty!"

"No?" The inspector's eyes were watching the younger man's face with a curious expression in their keen depths. Then, taking his pocket- book from his breast pocket, he carefully extracted a bank-note and held it out to Cardyn. "Do you know what this is?"

"A fifty-pound bank-note," replied Cardyn, glancing at it in surprise. "Do you mean that—"

"It is one of the notes given in payment for the pearls by Messrs. Spagnum and Thirgood's manager to the supposed Lady Anne Daventry. The first we have traced so far. It was paid to her dressmaker by—whom do you think?"

"Miss Balmaine, suppose," Bruce said quietly. "That is what you mean, is it not?"

"Not quite," said the inspector, a note of triumph creeping into his voice. "This note was paid to Madame Benoit by Miss Dorothy Fyvert in part payment of her account, which account had been running on for several years. Madame says that she had of late been very pressing for at least something on account, as her own liabilities were great. Another thread of the clue leading to Miss Dorothy Fyvert!"

"Clue—clue!" Bruce Cardyn repeated contemptuously. "If all the clues in the world led to Dorothy Fyvert I should still believe her innocent. As for this"—flicking the note contemptuously—"it is no clue at all. It may have been given to Miss Fyvert by Miss Balmaine, or by anybody. Probably it was a present from Lady Anne herself, for I am coming round to the opinion that the old lady sold her pearls and then pretended to have lost them."

"So that is your opinion, is it?" the inspector questioned dryly. "Well, well, time will show. Now, Mr. Cardyn, we have a busy day or two before us. This house is to be closed and placed in the hands of caretakers as soon as possible. As you know by Lady Anne's will, her brother has the right to select what furniture of hers he pleases up to the value of two hundred pounds, the rest passes to Mr. John Daventry, the jewels and Lady Anne's personal belongings are left to Miss Fyvert, though a codicil gives certain jewels to Miss Margaret Balmaine. Now, Mr. Fyvert and Mr. Daventry have decided that with a few exceptions the furniture shall be sold and the house placed in an agent's hands as soon as possible and either sold or let on a long lease. Mr. Daventry goes down to the Keep to-morrow and Mr. Fyvert and his nieces and Miss Balmaine will leave for North Coton at the end of the week. The servants are to be discharged at once. They will have their legacies and Mr. Daventry will give them a month's board and wages. Then, when the house is empty, our opportunity will come in. You and I will be able to do something, Mr. Cardyn."

"I don't know!" Bruce Cardyn took a few steps up the room then turned as if he had come to a sudden resolution. "If we have not discovered the murderer when the people are in the house I don't think we shall do much when it is empty. But, in any case, inspector, it is my intention to give up this case."

"Really! May I ask why?" The inspector took up a position with his back to the fire, throwing a lightning glance from time to time from beneath his bushy eyebrows at Cardyn.

"Well, in the first place, I am not really any use," Cardyn said, his voice growing determined. "I do not know whether it is by your orders, inspector, but any independent investigation attempt is at once suppressed by the police. I am reduced to watching you at your work and becoming a sort of chorus—a Watson to your Sherlock Holmes, don't you know. Now that won't suit me. I came here, engaged by Lady Anne Daventry herself, to make her life safe and to discover her would-be assassin. How lamentably I failed you know as well as I do. But acknowledging my failure I see now that I ought to have retired from the case, not stayed on as your assistant or factotum, whichever you like to call it."

"So now you want to leave me to finish the case, suppose."

"Yes. I mean to leave the case in the hands of the regular police. My partner is already grumbling at my long absence."

"Just so!" The inspector came a step nearer. "Suppose I say that you shall not go—that you shall stay and help us just as long as I choose, Mr. Bruce Cardyn?"

Cardyn flushed hotly.

"I cannot imagine anything so absurdly inconceivable."

"Can you not?" A change came into the inspector's voice. It grew suddenly stern and harsh. "And yet I say it now. I tell you that if you attempt to give up this case, I will have you instantly arrested for the murder of Lady Anne Daventry. You will stay with me and act as my assistant or factotum, as you term it, until I release you. Now, do you understand?" His steel-grey eyes were fixed gimlet-like upon the young man's face, as though they would wrest every secret his brain contained from him.

For a moment Bruce Cardyn stared at him in speechless stupefaction. Then the hot colour that anger had brought to his face during the first part of the inspector's speech paled suddenly. He became white, lurid, corpse-like. Only his eyes met the inspector's honestly enough, but with something— was it horror or fear or anguish, or some subtler emotion compounded of all three?—looking out of their tortured depths.

He moistened his lips, he tried to speak, but at first no words would come.

"You mean—you mean—what do you mean?" he stuttered at last.

The Ferret's eyes watched him mercilessly, missing not one detail, not one iota of the misery in his face. Then the inspector came close up to him.

"Now you shall hear what I mean," the grim voice went on. He stuck his face forward and whispered a few words in the young man's ear. "Now I think you know what I mean—and what other people will call you if I speak aloud—now you will realize why you will stay here as the Watson to my Sherlock Holmes, until I give you permission to return to your inquiry office—to retire from the case."

CHAPTER XI

THE PAPERS WERE FULL of the inquest on Lady Anne Daventry. There were sensational headlines on the front pages, developments were expected hourly. The inspector's remarks about the finger-prints were quoted everywhere. John Daventry's evidence was given almost verbatim.

A great pile of the morning papers lay on the breakfast table in that house in Charlton Crescent. A hurried perusal of them was being rapidly made by John Daventry, while the raucous cries of the street vendors, floating in through the open window, could be heard from the Bayswater Road.

"Finger-Print Test!" "Clues in the Hands of the Police!"

At last with an exclamation of rage Daventry strode to the window and banged it down.

The only other occupant of the room, the rector of North Coton, looked up in mild surprise from his breakfast.

"Dear me, John, what is the matter?"

"Matter?" echoed Daventry in exasperated accents. "Didn't you hear those confounded newsboys in the streets just now?"

"I am afraid I was not taking any notice of them," confessed the rector. "You see, my dear John, that is a fault I am afraid we priests are very prone to, inattention. We have so schooled ourselves, I might almost say as a duty, to abstract ourselves from our earthly surroundings when we are composing our sermons that it becomes almost second nature."

In spite of his wrath Daventry grinned wickedly. "I have taught myself to abstract my thoughts when I am listening to 'em, I know."

The rector's mild smile did not decrease.

"That is the sort of thing the rising generation thinks funny, I believe. Never mind, my dear John, time will bring you wisdom. And now, to change the subject. Personally I think that it is a mistake in talking so much of the five people in the room when my dear departed sister was murdered, and implying, or saying as some of them do say in so many words, that the murderer was to be found among you. The very idea would be ludicrous if the occasion was not so serious. The doors were open, and anyone might have come in and snatched up the dagger and—and used it and got away again. To say nothing of the man at the window—"

"Damn!" said John Daventry suddenly and heartily.

"My dear John!" The rector looked shocked.

"I beg your pardon, sir." Daventry pushed back his chair and going over to the mantelpiece took a cigarette from his case and lighted it. "But when I think of that blighter lose my temper. If he hadn't got up to the window with his clamps or whatever the things are he wears, Aunt Anne would have been alive now. Do you suppose anyone would have got into the room and stabbed her if we had all been sitting round at tea?"

"Of course they could not," agreed Mr. Fyvert. "I see you hold the theory of the Cat Burglar, John."

"What other theory is there to hold?" Daventry questioned. "The fellow was there safe enough. They tell me he couldn't have got up from the terrace, because there were detectives planted all about the garden below. Well, if those bally brutes in the garden were no better than their master in the house, don't think they would have done much to interfere with the Cat Burglar."

"I don't know—I don't know." The rector, having finished his breakfast, folded his hands over his slightly prominent waistcoat and looked at Daventry with friendly interest. "I have formed no theory at all myself. I am content to think of it as a terrible and mysterious happening, and to leave it at that, until all is revealed in due time."

"I tell you what, Mr. Fyvert, I have woke up two or three times in a night sometimes lately, and have seen the whole blasted thing—the scaffold and all the thingumajigs, you know, and feel that I have had a good breakfast—tea and toast and an egg—the poor beggars always do, you know. And I'm there all tied up and blindfolded. My God! I went over the trenches times enough, but this— And when I think of the poor wretches that have faced it—and women too—my Lord, but it won't bear thinking about." He ended with a strong shudder, and turning his face to the mantelpiece rested his arms on the high wooden shelf and laid his head upon his hands.

Mr. Fyvert looked at him with pitying wonder.

"My dear John, this is nerves, you know—nothing but nerves! You must make up your mind not to give way to it. It is a good thing you are going down to the Keep. In the country and away from this house you will soon look upon things in a different light."

"I don't know what sort of a light the folks at the Keep will regard me in," retorted Daventry. "They liked Aunt Anne down there, you know. They knew her before the boys died and she became crabby and crotchety. I would go abroad—big game shooting or something of that sort—but that fellow Furnival gave me a hint that if I tried to get out of reach in any way I should be arrested at once."

"I am inclined to think that Inspector Furnival exceeds his duty," observed Mr. Fyvert, stroking his clean-shaven chin. "He said something of the same kind to the girls this morning."

"The girls!" thundered Daventry, staring at him. "Do you mean Dorothy and Margaret?"

"Oh, do not shout so, my dear John. It goes through my head," the rector said, putting his hand to his brow. "I quite agree with you—the idea is preposterous. He was speaking more particularly to Margaret, I think. She was speaking of returning to Australia. I fancy that since my poor sister's death she has felt that she would rather go home to her old friends. One cannot wonder at it. But Furnival warned her that neither she nor any of the witnesses would be allowed to get out of communication with the police."

"Then I should think he does indeed exceed his duty," uttered Daventry explosively. "Of course if the police have reason to think that anybody committed a crime they can arrest him or her as the case may be. But I am blessed if they can keep the whole lot of us dangling round while they try to manufacture evidence against us. I shall consult my solicitor as soon as I get back to the Keep. I don't put any faith in these jumped-up johnnies here myself."

"I think you will be quite wise," the rector approved. "I suppose you know that Margaret is anxious to realize her share of what was left her by my sister."

"No, I didn't know. But I think—" Daventry was beginning, when he was interrupted.

Soames came in with a pile of letters that had come in by the second post.

"Might I speak to you, gentlemen, for a minute?" he said, looking inquiringly from one to the other.

There was no doubt that the tragedy of his mistress's death had told terribly upon Soames and was still telling upon him. He looked years older than the bland and portly butler who had taken the cakes in to that memorable tea-party.

"I wanted to ask you in the first place, gentlemen, if the house is to be closed from to-morrow, what is to become of my silver? Is it to go to the bank?"

"No. Nothing is to be taken from the house but your own personal belongings, I understand from Inspector Furnival," the rector of North Coton answered him, while Daventry stared moodily into the fire.

"But—but, sir, I can't leave it like that," expostulated Soames. "Some of it is very valuable and my lady set great store by it and it has always been my pride to keep it as she liked to see it. It would break my heart to leave it here, to be stolen by anybody who got into the house."

"The silver will be safe enough, Soames," John Daventry interposed. "The house will be occupied by men from Scotland Yard. But you must have your inventory ready. You will have to go over it with Inspector Furnival this afternoon, I expect."

"What, sir?" Soames started as if he had been stung, and a thin streak of red showed in his cheeks. "Go over my silver with Inspector Furnival as if I was a common thief? Me that has never laid a teaspoon wrong since I have been in her ladyship's service!"

"Ah, well! You are only in the same boat as the rest of us, Soames," Daventry said with a grim humour that was new to him. "We are all thieves and murderers in the eyes of the police."

"You always will have your joke, sir," Soames said with a sickly smile. "But, if I could have given it over to you, Mr. John, or to you, Mr. Fyvert, sir, instead of to the police, I should not have minded half so much. But to the police!"

"Well, well! Buck up, Soames, you will have to get over it. After all, it is left to different people, so you would have to part with it anyhow," Daventry went on. "But about yourself, Soames. What are you going to do, old chap? One doesn't like to think of you with anyone else, after all your years of faithful service with the Daventrys. But we have got old Grieve at the Keep, and my mother won't hear of anyone in his place."

"No. Nor is it right that she should, sir, if you will excuse me," Soames said respectfully. "But, if you would allow me, sir, I did hear when old Mr. Blount of the Daventry Arms died, that the widow wasn't going to keep the house on. If you would let it to me and speak a good word for me with the magistrates—"

"Oh, that would be all right, of course. Though I don't know how far my words would go with the magistrates nowadays. I am likely to find that out for myself soon, I fancy," John Daventry said with sardonic humour. "And of course we should love to have you at Daventry, old chap. But it will run into a good bit of money. Mrs. Blount wants to sell the furniture with the house, and there will be the transfer of the licence and Heaven knows what. Do you think you will be able to manage it?"

"I hope so, sir. I have always had good money, as you know. And I have been a thrifty man and put by a little each year, so with what her poor ladyship left me, I am quite well off. Besides—" he paused, smiling and looking sheepish.

"Besides what?" cried Daventry. "Upon my word, I believe you are going to be married, Soames! Who is it, man? Out with it—who is the lucky lady?"

"I look upon myself as the lucky one, sir," said Soames, striving to recapture his usual manner and failing signally. "But we have walked out for years, though nothing binding between us, and now we are thinking of spending our old age together. I speak of Miss Pirnie, sir—her late ladyship's maid."

"Pirnie, by Jove!" For once John Daventry's laugh rang out almost as free from cares as ever as a vision of the lady maid's mincing affectation, and her elaborately coiffured dyed hair, rose before his eyes. Then he held out his hand. "I wish you the best of luck, Soames, both of you. You may depend upon me about the Daventry Arms. We should like to have you settled near as neighbours of ours."

"Thank you, sir. Thank you, sir!" There were real tears in Soames's eyes as he pressed John's hand and then turned to press that which the rector of North Coton extended in congratulation. "You are very kind. And if you ever want a hand at the Keep, sir, why, we shall always be pleased to do what we can, speaking for Miss Pirnie and myself, for we shall always look upon ourselves as the Daventrys' servants."

When he had bowed himself out, John Daventry looked at Mr. Fyvert.

"Good old Soames! Well, I am glad Aunt Anne's money is going to make those two good souls happy."

"Indeed, yes!" responded the rector. "Soames belongs to the old-fashioned class of servant—a type that is rapidly becoming extinct nowadays."

CHAPTER XII

Mosswolds' was one of those very small, ultra-smart, restaurants that are to be found tucked away in side-streets all about the West End; mostly perhaps in the region of Bond Street and the shops. No band played. Mosswolds' did not cater for the class of person who takes tea to the accompaniment of a jazz band. But the table linen and the china were always fresh and dainty. Flowers from the country came up every morning to Mosswolds' and were set in crystal vases on every table. Above there was plenty of space. The tables stood in corners, or by the windows, or in the middle of the room, but always the customers could talk without fear of being overheard. To-day at four o'clock, there were very few people in the room, but then Mosswolds' was never crowded. The waitresses wore a particularly becoming uniform of pale almond green, with cream-coloured mob caps and dainty coquettish aprons. The frocks were short enough to show silk stockings of the same shade of green, and suede shoes to match with Louis Quinze heels and paste buckles. Report had it that all the waitresses at Mosswolds' were ladies. However that might be, they were generally remarkably good-looking girls.

This afternoon, as business was slack, one of them was talking to a customer who had just come in. A well-dressed woman of middle-age who seemed to be waiting for some one. Presently a young man entered; a tall, rather good-looking man with fair hair and a monocle screwed into his left eye. He selected a table near the window and sat down.

The woman who had been talking to the waitress moved to a table at the other side of the room, quite out of earshot, but from whence a good view of the second customer's table could be obtained.

Then she ordered tea, and, taking out a book, began glancing at it in an absent fashion.

The young man, too, ordered tea, and then began to watch the door. Quite evidently he was expecting some one; more than once he glanced impatiently at the clock. At last a girl in deep mourning came quickly through the swing door. He rose quickly and went forward to meet her.

"My darling, I thought I was never going to see you again!"

"Oh, Davy dear, you know it hasn't been my fault!" the girl said quickly. "And even now I can't stop long. But—is this safe?" She looked round doubtfully. A few people sat about at distant tables. Just opposite was the friend of the waitress. Upon her the girl's glance rested longest. "You are sure she can't hear?"

The man laughed. "Quite, quite sure. Come along, sweetheart, we are as safe as houses here. And I have promised the waitress a considerable *douceur* not to let anyone come near us."

They sat down and began to talk, leaning forward and looking into each other's eyes in a fashion that made the waitress giggle. The woman at the opposite table smiled a little too, as she put down her book and began to attack the pile of buttered toast she had ordered.

The two at the table went on talking.

"Why didn't you come to the old place yesterday or the day before?" the man questioned.

"Because that horrid detective was prying about," answered the girl, whom the distant watcher had no difficulty in identifying as Margaret Balmaine. "He is always popping up somewhere, just in the last place one expects him. It is a marvel I have been able to get away from him today. Even now I shouldn't be surprised if he were the next person to come through that door. Davy, are we going to North Coton to-morrow?"

"So I have heard. At least I know you are leaving town to-morrow. Your destination is at present a secret, so far as the press is concerned. You will be glad to get away, darling!"

"Glad!" the girl echoed. "Oh, Davy, life at Charlton Crescent just now is nothing but hell! Picture it. Every one looking at every one else, wondering who is guilty—who may be the next one to be killed. And detectives all around us spying, trying to find out the smallest thing to tell them who the murderer is." She bit her lip. "I don't know what to do—I'm frightened! Frightened. And—and, Davy"—her voice dropped to the faintest whisper—"suppose they suspect us?" A great pity dawned in the man's eyes. Ordinarily David Branksome's face was hard, his expression unsympathetic. Only one woman ever saw the softening in his eyes, heard the tenderness in his tone.

"They couldn't suspect, my darling—you—we are safe enough. And very soon we shall be away from it all, alone together, just you and I."

A new light dawned in the girl's eyes. She bent a little nearer.

"Ah! yes! think of that time, Davy, dream of it. And yet"—her face clouding over as suddenly as it had brightened—"something seems to tell me that it will never come, that he—that man will find out. Oh, Davy, Davy, in spite of all we have done, all our precautions, suppose he—he finds it out. What will they do to me if he does?" She broke off with a gasp of horror.

The man leaned over and laid one hand on hers. "They won't find out," he said tenderly. "They can't, I have been much too careful, and—and if the very worst came, should speak out, I should not let you suffer."

The girl gazed at him with terrified eyes. "But—but don't you know that that would be worse than anything for me—that I would a thousand times sooner bear the penalty myself. Oh, Davy, Davy, will you never understand?"

"I know that you have always been far too good for me," the man said, his hard voice breaking. "Ah, darling, if you had never met me how different your life might have been."

"No life would have been life to me without you!" the girl said unsteadily. "I don't mind anything, Davy, if they don't separate us."

"They shall not!" the man assured her. But somehow his confident tone did not ring true. "Be brave just a little while longer," he went on, "it can hardly be a week or two now, and then think of the reward. I keep it before my eyes always."

"So do I!" the girl whispered. "But—but I don't know how long it will be, Davy. I can't get Mr. Fyvert to tell me even when he thinks things will be settled up. He keeps saying that the manner of Lady Anne's death complicates matters. I believe the police tell him to. Davy, you will come to see me at North Coton?"

"I—don't know!" the man hesitated. "We shall have to find some means of communication, of course. But there is always the possibility that our being seen together may delay matters, or even bring about—discovery!"

"I don't see why it should!" the girl said obstinately. "It is bad enough being alone among strangers, knowing what I know. But to be there, to look at one another, to catch some one looking at you sideways. Oh, Davy, Davy, never can you imagine the horror. Often I think I shall go mad, shall tell them—"

"Oh, no!" The man's eyes narrowed; he drew his thin lips together. "You must be my own brave girl to the end. Think what it means, darling. The success, the reward of all our efforts. No more struggling. No more separation. And it will not be for so long as you fear. Did you tell Mr. Fyvert that you wished to go back to Australia?"

"Yes, yes, I did, but it was of no use," the girl said wearily. "I do not think he would mind me realizing my share and going back. But at the present time the police would not allow anyone to leave the country—anyone, that is to say, who may be wanted as a witness at the inquest, or any subsequent proceedings."

He drew his brows together. "That cannot go on for ever. The English law would not give them the power to keep you indefinitely, I am certain. And the moment they have paid the money over—"

"But—but if we do get away," the girl whispered. "If—if they find out anything afterwards nowadays they could follow us to Australia. There is the wireless and aeroplanes and all sorts of things, we shouldn't be safe anywhere."

The man dropped his voice to a caressing murmur. "Only we shouldn't go to Australia! What a little goose you are, darling; I know the sweetest spot on earth and all my arrangements are made. When our—I shall say our—honeymoon is over, I wonder how you will like to be a farmer's wife?"

The girl's face lighted up momentarily. "I think, perhaps, I might like it very much—if you were the farmer," she confessed.

"It won't be as dull as it sounds," the man went on. "We shall have our gay times and life can be very jolly in those southern republics."

"Gaiety—gaiety! I only want safety—and you!" the passion in her voice quickening. "But, Davy," coming nearer and speaking so that he could only catch the words with difficulty—"will you tell me if you—whether you—"

"Hush!" The man's voice broke sharply across her hesitating speech. "Don't ask—don't want to know anything. Remember that walls have ears—"

The girl stood up shivering, drawing her furs more closely round her.

"Then—then I must go now. I have been longer than I ought. Suppose Dorothy has finished with her dressmaker and gone home?"

"Does she know?"

The girl shook her head. "No! But I think perhaps she guesses a little. She was busy looking at patterns and I just slipped away and left her a message saying I had a bad toothache and had gone to get something for it. Still I think she will wait. She is not a bad sort—Dorothy. And some day I hope things will be straight for her."

"Of course they will," the man assented. But his eyelids flickered curiously, his narrow lips curled in an unpleasant fashion as he spoke. He pushed his chair back. "And I suppose I must not even see you home, Margaret?"

"No! No! somebody might recognize us and guess!"

She looked very attractive standing there, her heavy furs drawn closely round her shoulders, her throat gleaming white between, the deep red gold of her hair just peeping out from beneath her cloche hat, her eyes looking all the bigger and clearer for the dark half circles beneath them, for the touch of lassitude and fatigue that gave her face the look of pathos that enhanced the beauty that was at times hard and unsympathetic. Her breathing had quickened; despite her furs one could see her breast rising and falling, even the plentiful use of her lipstick could not altogether spoil the perfect curves of her mouth—the shape of her pretty lips.

The eyes of the man watching seemed to drink in every detail of her loveliness. "Darling!" he said hoarsely at last. "Don't forget, child. Don't let John Daventry—"

The girl drew up her small golden head. "John Daventry is nothing to me," she said icily. "If, after all, you do not trust me, Davy!"

"I trust you with everything," the man said with sudden fire, "even with life itself."

Several people were coming in. A little group gathered in the middle of the room and obstructed the view of the watcher on the side opposite. When once more she could see clearly the girl had gone, the man was sitting alone at the table. He beckoned to the waitress and put the bill into her hand with what was evidently an unusually liberal tip, to judge by her expression.

The watcher got up and paid her modest account.

"I shall always be thankful that my mother made me learn the lip language when was a child," she said to herself as she went out.

CHAPTER XIII

"And now," said Inspector Furnival, "there is a little hard work before us, Mr. Cardyn, if we want to elucidate the mystery of Charlton Crescent."

Bruce Cardyn did not attempt to answer this thrust. Of late he had not been thinking so much of the dead Lady Anne Daventry as of the live Dorothy Fyvert. For Dorothy had been as good as her word. Ever since she had discovered Cardyn to be a detective she had deliberately cold-shouldered him, she had never spoken to him unless absolutely compelled, and she had taken pains to express her contempt for his chosen calling, whenever possible. Yet for that very reason perhaps Cardyn's thoughts dwelt on her persistently. She had dominated them more or less ever since the night of the fire; he had not realized himself to how great an extent until he met her again in

Charlton Crescent. Then what had been heretofore a cherished memory became a living, breathing reality—the goddess of his dreams had become a very woman.

Inspector Furnival smiled as he looked at him.

"Come now, Mr. Cardyn, you must rouse yourself. There are just a few questions I should like you to consider with me before we set to work. I wonder if you can form an idea what they are."

Cardyn shook his head wearily. "Probably my ideas would not coincide with yours."

"Well, come in here and I will show you my list. You can see how you would answer them." The inspector opened the library door as he spoke.

The house was now entirely in the hands of the police. They had just watched the dispersal of the household. John Daventry had gone down to the Keep in his small touring car, taking with him Soames who was about to apply for the transfer of the licence of the Daventry Arms. Mr. and Mrs. Fyvert had been accompanied to North Coton by their two nieces, with Margaret Balmaine and their respective maids. The other servants had dispersed in different directions, all leaving their addresses with the police. Though none of the furniture had gone the house looked cold and dismantled in the absence of the life and movement that had so recently pervaded it.

Cardyn shivered as he followed Inspector Furnival. The library was the only room in the house that looked much the same as usual. Since Lady Anne's death it had become the headquarters of the police, and Inspector Furnival's papers were strewn about, while books, presumably on subjects in the inspector's mind, lay on the table.

The inspector took his favourite chair and, drawing a sheet of foolscap towards him, wrote:

"Question 1. Did Lady Anne Daventry herself sell her pearls to Messrs. Spagnum, or did some one impersonate her sufficiently cleverly to deceive their manager?

"Question 2. Who engineered the man at the window?"

Cardyn bent forward as the inspector's capable fingers wrote down the second.

"Engineered?" he questioned.

"Yes—um, well, yes!" The inspector tapped his lip with his pencil. "Perhaps 'engineered' is not the proper word, and yet it describes what I mean better than 'managed' or 'helped.'"

"But do you mean that some one in the house knew—helped?" Bruce questioned.

"In the house or not—I do!" the inspector said firmly. "Why, put it to yourself, Mr. Cardyn. How could any man get up to that window and get away again without being seen unless he had the help of some one! How he did it is sufficiently difficult of explanation, even with the help.

"Question 3. Who made the footmarks on the border, under the window at the back of the hall?

"When those three questions are answered, Mr. Cardyn, we shall be in a position to say who stabbed Lady Anne Daventry, as I firmly believe."

"Ah, when!" Bruce Cardyn echoed, looking at them.

"And now," the inspector went on, "the first thing we have to do is to make a thorough and systematic search of the house. I think we will begin with the rooms of the two young ladies. But first let me show you this." He took a sheet of paper from his pocket-book and handed it to Cardyn.

The young man's heart beat fast as he saw the writing: "The fifty-pound note about which you were inquiring," Dorothy had written curtly, "was given me last week as my half-yearly allowance, by my aunt, Lady Anne Daventry—"

"What do you think of that?" the inspector inquired.

"I am quite certain that whatever Miss Fyvert tells you is true," Bruce Cardyn said steadily.

"Quite so, quite so!" The inspector's eyes twinkled as he watched the young man's moody face. "You understand, of course, that this is one of the notes paid by Messrs. Spagnum and Thirgood to the real or supposed Lady Anne Daventry?"

"I recognized that at once!" assented Cardyn. "And that answers your first question. Lady Anne must have sold the pearls herself since she gave part of the price to Miss Fyvert."

"Oh, oh! Is that all you have to say, Mr. Cardyn?" the inspector questioned ironically. "I do not think matters will be settled quite so quickly as that. But now to the bedrooms—Miss Balmaine's first."

Margaret Balmaine had occupied a large bedroom on the landing above Lady Anne's. Like the rest of the house it was furnished in Victorian fashion—a big four-poster, a massive wardrobe, a large mahogany dressing-table with a big oval mirror inset; the chairs, the couch and the washstand were all of the same heavy type. Apparently Miss Balmaine had not troubled to make any changes. The only traces of her occupancy that a cursory glance revealed were sundry empty bottles on the toilet table, and a few ashes in the empty fireplace, and an incongruous note was struck by the presence of a small sewing-machine on a side table.

The inspector began to search the room in a very systematic manner. Every shelf, every drawer in the sewing-machine, even every peg in the wardrobe was moved. Every bottle was opened, every small box, every inch of the furniture and bedstead scrutinized. In one thing only, as far as they could see, had Lady Anne been up-to-date with in her bedrooms. Instead of the all-over carpet of Victorian days, the floors were stained and there were soft rugs spread at the bedside and before the fireplace. At last the inspector paused.

"Not much to be learned here?"

"The fireplace!" Cardyn had got out his microscope. The inspector had his in his hand. Together they knelt down, but the ashes were just ashes of wood and coal, that was all. When they had finished, the inspector stood up.

"Well, sometimes there is as much to be learned from what you don't find in a person's room as from what you do."

Bruce made no answer. He regarded this meticulous search of Margaret Balmaine's room as entirely superfluous. The inspector drew up the bottom sash of the window and leaned out, looking upwards and downwards and twisting himself about this way and that, so that he could get a good view sideways. The creepers on this side of the house grew right up to the window-sills and had been parted so as to climb up each side.

Inspector Furnival stretched out and plucked a large ivy leaf from just below the ledge.

"Miss Balmaine evidently thought it so important to destroy all trace of what she burned that she even gathered the ashes together and threw them out of the window," he remarked as he displayed a slight powdering of white ash upon the ivy leaf.

"No hope of finding out what was burnt from that. But as said before we may gather a good deal from the fact that it was burned. But come, want to have a look at Lady Anne's bedroom." He led the way to the big room below.

Cardyn followed, mildly wondering. It seemed to him that they had gone through every inch of this room over and over again already. Lady Anne's furniture in her own room was even more Victorian than in the rest of the house. The four-poster, with its carefully calendered chintz hangings, seemed to belong to an even earlier period. There were no gimcrack ornaments or bottles of essences or cosmetics in her room, nothing but a few solid boxes and two very large, beautifully cut crystal scent-bottles much like the looking-glass.

The inspector did not waste much time. He went straight to the wardrobe where Lady Anne's dresses were and threw open the door. Modern fashions and post-war tendencies had affected Lady Anne not one whit. John Daventry had once said of her that had crinolines been worn when she was young she would have been wearing them at the time of her death. As it was she wore the long flounced dresses, the fichus, the corsets, the leg of mutton sleeves, and the tightly-fitting bodices of the late Victorian era. Her dress had been simplified by the fact that since her boys' death she had worn nothing but black. In the long drawers reposed her fine old laces, a couple of Indian shawls, dainty cobwebby linen and silk undergarments—her gowns in various stages of wear were hanging in the big middle compartment. The inspector made straight for this division and dived in, to emerge a moment later with a triumphant expression.

"Yesterday I counted eight gowns, to-day—to-day there are nine."

"What do you say?" Cardyn was regarding him with a distinctly sceptical expression. "Where should the ninth come from, pray?"

"The ninth," said the inspector, taking out the garments one by one and laying them on the bed, "was worn by the woman who impersonated Lady Anne at Spagnum and Thirgood's."

"If there was such a woman," Bruce questioned, "why should she put her gown here?"

"To get rid of it of course," the inspector said, with what Bruce usually termed his air of cocksureness. "Don't you remember that every one in the house was likely to have his or her luggage searched? I had some such eventuality as this in my mind when I framed that order. You see the possession of a gown of this kind would inevitably have damned the possessor. It was too bulky to be hidden or burned. This I call a brilliant idea for disposing of it. It might have succeeded, probably would have, if the idea of making a note of the number of dresses in Lady Anne's wardrobe had not occurred to me yesterday. Now, to discover the interloper."

He turned back to the bed and began to examine the garments minutely.

Cardyn watched him for a moment. "I am not supposing you made a mistake in the number of dresses yesterday. But it is surely possible that the maid transferred another gown of Lady Anne's to the wardrobe?"

"She hadn't the chance!" the inspector said as his quick, capable fingers turned the garments over. "Pirnie went early yesterday afternoon, you may remember. There was nothing to keep her— her work was over. I went over to the wardrobe after she was gone."

"Then this was only put in last night!"

The inspector nodded. "And I should have caught the person who did it in the act, but the child Maureen had an attack of sleep-walking and I followed her. A good thing I did, for she seemed to be trying to throw herself out of the window. Her sister was terrified."

"Which window?" Cardyn questioned quickly.

"The one at the back of the landing over this," the inspector answered, throwing another gown back. "These damned things look all alike and we shall have to get a dressmaking expert here."

"I believe they always have the name of the woman that made them stuck on somewhere—on a bit of tape, don't you know?" ventured Cardyn. "Now, if one of these was different from the others it might tell us something."

"Brainy idea!" commented the inspector. "But unfortunately every one of these gowns has the name of Lady Anne's dressmaker upon it. What do you make of that?"

"It looks to me as if you were on the wrong track," Cardyn commented. "I should say they were all Lady Anne's."

"Would you indeed!" the inspector questioned in that satiric voice of his that seemed to be reserved for Cardyn.

He had taken a small case from his pocket and was looking intently at what looked like a snippet of black rag laid across.

"I suppose you are wondering where this came from?" As Bruce did not reply, he went on, "It was caught in a little bit of the side of the table on which Miss Balmaine's sewing-machine stands."

"A—h!" Bruce drew a long breath. "Still—"

"In itself it is nothing. But Miss Balmaine burned something, remember, and there would be bonnet and mantle to get rid of. This tiny bit of silk is almost too small to make certain, but I believe it is exactly the same texture as this gown," pointing to the one that lay by itself.

Bruce put the piece of silk on the skirt of the gown and examined it through his microscope. "I believe it is. You see this gown is much thicker than some of the others. It is what is called watered silk—and on this little piece I see a suspicion of the water."

"Well done!" said the inspector absently.

But he did not appear to be much excited at the discovery. He was holding the gown up at arm's length, shaking it and peering into the folds.

He drew out a tiny bit of notepaper, a scrap that had evidently once been part of a letter.

"Ah! at last we have caught our clever friend napping!" he exclaimed triumphantly. "'Impossible to come to you, my sweetheart, until suspicion has—'" That was all. On the other side of the paper was nothing, and not another scrap of paper was to be found, search and shake as the inspector would. At last he desisted and turned to Cardyn. "I suppose that you will hardly assert that this belonged to Lady Anne."

"Well, no," Bruce conceded. "But unfortunately it does not seem to bear any internal evidence as to the real owner."

The inspector chuckled and apparently he was well pleased with the result of his search so far.

"It may help us—we are getting the threads together. What is that?" as a loud rat-tat and peal of the bell sounded simultaneously through the house. "A telegram! Can't be from the Yard. They would have phoned!" the inspector grumbled.

Cardyn hurried downstairs to the door, a vague sense of disaster deepening as he went.

CHAPTER XIV

THE BROWN ENVELOPE was addressed to Inspector Furnival. Leaving the boy on the steps, Cardyn took the telegram to the inspector and stood by whilst he opened it.

"From Dorothy Fyvert, The Rectory, North Coton," he read aloud. Then he uttered a sharp exclamation of surprise: "What does this mean?"

"What is it, man? Can't you say?" Cardyn questioned hoarsely.

"'Maureen has disappeared. Is she with you? If not, make inquiries. Coming up by next train,'" the inspector read out slowly and stutteringly. "Disappeared! That child! But when, or where. It is all very well to say 'Make inquiries,' but how is one to make inquiries if one has no data to start from?"

"Better phone to North Coton at once," Cardyn suggested.

The inspector shook his head. "No use. They are not on the phone at North Coton Rectory. I had to wire when Lady Anne died. The Rev. Augustus said he wouldn't be bothered with one for anything. I fancy he rather despises modern improvements—like his sister. 'Coming up by next train?' Now, I wonder what that means? We will have a look at the time-table."

He turned to "Bradshaw."

"Um! This telegram has been delayed," he said grimly, as he turned over the pages. "Three-quarters of an hour longer than it should have been on the way. Ah, here it is. There is a train from Overend, the Junction for North Coton, due at Marylebone directly. If Miss Fyvert caught that she could be here in a few minutes.

"Oh, no good going to meet it," in answer to a murmur from Cardyn. "We should only miss one another; pass on the road. But what can have gone wrong with the child? However, it's no use speculating until we know the facts of the disappearance. Now, until they come I think we will just take a look round the offices, the butler's pantry, the kitchens and the servants' hall."

"There didn't seem to be much there when we went over them before," remarked Cardyn.

"No; and I don't expect to find much there now," the inspector nodded. "If there ever was anything incriminating in the rooms, it would have been got rid of before now you may be sure." He spoke as if he had entirely forgotten he was talking to one of the suspected number.

Cardyn shot a quick glance at him and a slow, dull crimson line showed on his forehead.

They went down the passage at the end of which was the green baize door admitting to the servants' quarters. The butler's pantry, which they visited first, was in absolute order. Soames's grief at parting with his beloved silver had led him to leave it in the most wonderful condition.

"Poor old Soames!" Cardyn remarked. "I hope he will get to the Daventry Arms all right. I don't think you will find anything here, inspector."

"Very likely not," the inspector assented. He was diving about in the cupboards and the waste-paper baskets. A scrap of paper seemed to have a fatal fascination for him. He spent the minutes Cardyn was restlessly counting, looking for Dorothy Fyvert's appearance, in examining with microscopic care a heap of old boots thrown carelessly in one of the corners.

"What are you looking for there?" Cardyn inquired impatiently at last.

"A pair of shoes—size eight," he answered, proceeding with his search, while Cardyn stared in mingled consternation and surprise.

But at the end of half an hour's search the inspector stood up. "Nothing to be done here to-day, anyhow. It is getting time those people were here—and, by Jove, they are!" as they heard a taxi stop before the front door, and an almost simultaneous ring.

Both men hurried back to the hall. Dorothy was on the top step. The inspector frowned as he saw that behind her stood Margaret Balmaine and the rector of North Coton.

"This bids fair to upset my apple-cart very considerably," he ejaculated.

Dorothy literally sprang in and caught his hands. "Maureen, has she been here?"

"Not a sign of her! Not a word but your telegram. Now, Miss Fyvert, just tell me as quickly and as quietly as you can what has happened!"

The inspector stepped back as he spoke; the others followed and stood round him, Margaret Balmaine slipping her arm through Dorothy's.

Both girls looked white and frightened. Dorothy was trembling from head to foot, her great brown eyes were full of tears.

"Oh, inspector, you will find her for me. Our mother left her in my charge." Her voice broke.

The inspector patted her hand. "I know just how bad you are feeling, Miss Fyvert. I am a family man, you know." He produced his notebook. "Now, you say the child has disappeared—where from?"

"We—we don't know," Dorothy cried. "When we got to North Coton Rectory, she just wasn't there—that was all."

"When did you see her last?"

"At Overend Junction," Dorothy answered, keeping back her emotion by a supreme effort.

Cardyn, watching, could see the muscles in her pretty throat pulsing and throbbing.

"She wouldn't come in the carriage with us. She would travel with the maids, and the doctor said she was to be contradicted as little as possible and, as it didn't seem to matter much, I let her go. At Overend we changed to the little branch to North Coton. It is a big, noisy Junction, and, as I had a lot of things to worry me, I thought Maureen was safe enough with the maids; and I did not look for her at North Coton Station. I shall reproach myself for ever that did not. But Mrs. Fyvert was taken ill in the train and we were all busy looking after her. Naturally, the maids believed that Maureen was in our compartment, while we thought she was with them. It was not until we were in the hall at the Rectory that I asked for her and found that nobody knew where she was. Uncle Augustus saw her at Overend just before the train started."

"I think I saw her then, my dear," corrected the rector. "It is my impression that I did. But my mind is much preoccupied just now, so that I should not like to say more. Still, I believe that one of the maids—"

"Yes, yes. Susan, my maid," Dorothy said feverishly. "She says that Maureen was with them at Overend, but that while she was looking after the luggage the child slipped away. The only clue we have at all to her disappearance is that Susan remarked that she saw some one on the platform very like Alice. You remember the housemaid that Maureen was so fond of. Oh, Inspector Furnival, can you find her for us?"

The inspector blew his nose vigorously. "Of course we shall find her. We will start at once. One moment—" He went into the library to the telephone. "That is all right," he said, coming back. "I have called up the police at Overend and put them on the track, and also given directions to one of our best men to go down at once. It ought not to be a difficult matter, though I wish we had not lost so much time at the outset."

"I didn't think we had," Dorothy said ruefully. "My first thought was to send that wire to you." The inspector gave a queer smile. "Yes, but that did not give us many particulars to work upon. However, all's well that ends well, and I expect we shall be able to restore Miss Maureen to you safe and sound within the next few hours."

"Oh, inspector, you really think so!"

All Dorothy's hard-won composure gave way now, and she burst into sobs.

The inspector patted her hand again. "There! There! you must not fret. Everything will come out all right in the end. And now to think where the child would be likely to go. You have another sister, Miss Fyvert?"

"Yes. Mrs. St. John Lavis—my half-sister, really. My mother was twice married. But Maureen would not go to her. She has seen very little of her of late years, and they never got on very well. Besides, Mrs. Lavis is abroad just now."

"You speak of the child's liking for this Alice Gray," the inspector questioned abruptly. "What was the secret of it?"

"Secret! There couldn't be any secret about it," Dorothy said. "Lady Anne appointed Alice to wait upon Maureen while she was here in the holidays, and the child took a fancy to her—that was all. Maureen was always capricious in her likes and dislikes."

"I thought it was a very curious liking myself," Margaret Balmaine observed, speaking for the first time. "And I must say that of late Maureen looked as if she were frightened to death. It was not only that she was ill, but she was scared—scared to death! She used to be the jolliest, liveliest little thing on earth—too jolly for me, a good deal. But lately there didn't seem to be a bit of spirit left in her. I shall always say it was very wrong to keep her in this house after Lady Anne's death. It has been a terrible atmosphere for us all. It must have been appalling for a delicate child like Maureen."

"But Maureen was never considered delicate," Dorothy contradicted. "And the police wouldn't have let me go until yesterday, or Alice. And the very idea of leaving us was enough to send Maureen into a frenzy. Besides everybody was strictly forbidden to speak to her of Aunt Anne's death."

"Not much use forbidding children to gossip with servants, as far as my experience goes," Miss Balmaine contradicted. "I remember, when I was a child staying in Derby, that spent half my time gossiping with the servants while my governess was away."

"Ah, yes. A fine old town, Derby," the inspector said in a bland tone that those who knew the Ferret best meant mischief. "I know that part of the country very well myself. It is a beautiful old town. Then you were in England when you were a child, Miss Balmaine?"

Was it a spasm of fear that shot over Margaret Balmaine's face? Even the inspector watching her between his narrowed eyelids could not tell. If it were, she recovered herself in a moment.

"England!" she repeated with a light laugh. "No, I never was in England until a few months ago. I thought you knew that, inspector. Oh, I see! it was my saying Derby that misled you. Derby is the name of the settlement nearest to us at that time at home. Just a tiny, tiny place, while I believe Derby in England is, as you say, a beautiful old town. There is a Melbourne in England too, I understand—quite a small place, while Melbourne in Australia is one of our great, magnificent cities. Funny, isn't it? Things seem topsy-turvy, don't they?"

"They often do in life!" the inspector said dryly. "But now to return to Miss Maureen. The first thing want is a detailed description of her, please, Miss Fyvert. Now her full name—"

"Mary Frances Adelaide Fyvert. But she has always been called Maureen. She was eleven last October."

The inspector was writing rapidly in his notebook. "Appearance, please—colour of eyes and hair, height. Has she any birth, or otherwise distinguishing mark?"

Dorothy bit her lips. "No, I don't believe she has the least little mark anywhere. Height—well, I am really not quite sure. About five feet, I should think, shouldn't you, inspector? But I'm not sure, people always said Maureen was tall for her age."

"We must try and get something a little more definite than that," the inspector said sharply. "Now, the colouring, please."

"She was fair and rosy, with big, hazel eyes and thick fair hair, bobbed. At least she used to be rosy," Dorothy corrected herself. "She has become terribly pale since she became ill."

"Clothing next, please—was it marked?"

"Just a short little frock of black marocain, with a black cloth coat, edged with real astrakan, and a little pull-on black hat. No, nothing would be marked, except her underclothing of course. That would be marked either 'Maureen' in an embroidered medallion or a monogram 'M.F.A.F.'"

"I see, thank you, Miss Fyvert." The inspector shut his notebook with a snap. "And now we must set to work to find her for you."

"And do you think you will, inspector?" Dorothy clasped her hands together, tears were vibrating in her voice, but it was evident that she was making a tremendous effort to retain her self-possession.

"Oh, what can have become of her?" she cried. "Mother's little Maureen whom she trusted to me. Surely, surely, nobody would be so cruel as to hurt a child."

"Oh, I don't think Miss Maureen has been hurt," the inspector assured her. "But now we will not waste time in suppositions. Mr. Fyvert—"

The rector answered the look. "I have wired to the Charlton Hotel for rooms. If you want us you will find us there, inspector. Now then, girls!" He took Dorothy's hand and beckoned to Margaret Balmaine.

As they reached the door, Dorothy pulled herself a little from him. "Uncle Augustus, surely there is an evil spell over this unhappy house! Why should these dreadful things be happening, one after the other—unless God has given us over to the power of the devil?"

When they had all gone, the inspector turned to Cardyn. "I feel inclined to echo Miss Fyvert's question. It is impossible this child's disappearance can be connected in any way with the horrible crime we are investigating, and yet—"

"Is it impossible?" Cardyn questioned quietly.

The inspector looked at him. "What do you mean?"

"I—really hardly know." Cardyn said slowly. "But I seem to have just a vague glimmering idea —that it might be. And yet it seems too improbable to be true."

CHAPTER XV

INSPECTOR FURNIVAL walked slowly along past the chairs by the Achilles statue, then he hesitated a moment and glanced round.

A poorly-dressed little lad ran up to him.

"Paper, sir?"

The inspector stooped to make his selection.

"Well?"

"Just a little further on, sir, up by the Row," the boy answered, his undertone to the full as cautious as the inspector's. "Near the first big clump of crocuses. She is sitting on a chair by herself and looks as if she was expecting some one."

The inspector gave him a nod and a copper and walked off briskly, paper in hand. He had not far to go. The solitary figure of a woman in mourning of which he was in search was close at hand. With a throb of satisfaction he saw that the only chair near her was empty. He slackened his pace a little as he went up, and raised his hat.

"Why, Miss Pirnie, this is an unexpected pleasure. Just having an hour or so off, as you may say, I thought I would turn into the park and have a look at the spring flowers. But it is dreary work taking one's enjoyment by oneself. So, if you will allow me—" He brought his chair close up to her, and sitting down with a hand on each knee he regarded her with a friendly smile.

Pirnie did not return the smile. She cast a frightened glance at him and half rose, then, changing her mind, sat down again.

But she made no attempt to respond to the inspector's civility. Instead she said abruptly:

"What do you want with me?"

The inspector's smile became more suave and childlike than ever.

"Want with you!" he echoed. "What should I want but a chat with a lady I have often admired? We detectives are pretty much like other men in our off-hours, Miss Pirnie."

The lady's maid was gradually recovering her self-possession. The inspector's manner was so friendly, his glance so respectful that her fears were allayed. She tossed her head now.

"I dare say! But—is this one of your off-hours then, Mr. Furnival?"

"Well, it looks like it, doesn't it?" The inspector stretched out his legs and regarded his feet contemplatively. "I must say I have no fancy for going off by myself for my bits of holidays. I like to see something of life—a scene like this now," waving his hand comprehensively at the passers-by.

"You don't spend them with your wife, then?" Pirnie pursued curiously and principally conscious of a monkey-like desire to annoy the inspector.

"Spend them with my wife! Good Lord, ma'am!" The inspector turned from his scrutiny of his boots to stare at her. "Ah, I see you don't know that I lost my poor wife three years ago. She left me with six children that have taken some looking after. But my favourite sister got married to a rogue, more years ago than I care to count. After he had broken her heart, he went off with another woman and she has made her home with me ever since and looked after the kids. She is very good to them, but it isn't altogether a satisfactory arrangement. In point of fact I have not married again, but it's quite on the cards I may, though I often think a man in my profession is best unmarried. If he is married, it is a job to keep things from a wife, leastways if he is attached to her, and that is what I should hope to be to mine."

It was a long speech for the Ferret, who was one of the most laconic of men in private life. At its conclusion he sat silent, looking straight before him with a pensive expression that accorded but ill with his sharp little features.

Pirnie bridled. A well-pleased smile lighted up her face. Her long black ear-rings shook, various odd little pieces of jewellery pinned about her black frock twinkled.

"Ay! It is one thing to say so beforehand, and another thing to stick to it afterwards."

"Well, well; it may be so," the inspector admitted cautiously. "But it seems to me the difficulty would be in not sticking to it, if it was the right woman."

The style of conversation was quite to Pirnie's liking. She began to think that she had sadly misused her opportunities hitherto. She had hardly cast a glance at Inspector Furnival— yet here was he an obvious victim to her charms. The inspector saw that his prey would be an easy one. He cast an admiring glance at her made-up countenance.

"I was just wondering—it isn't often I take a holiday and when I do I want to enjoy myself—I was wondering whether you would come and have a cup of tea with me. There is a tea place in Ridley street, off Knightsbridge, where they do you very well."

Surprise kept Pirnie silent for a minute, and the inspector went on.

"Ay! It has come to me that you wouldn't hesitate if it was Mr. Soames asking you. Well, well, it has been my luck to be just too late in other ways."

Pirnie flushed up unbecomingly, her markings showing in ghastly contrast with the dull crimson of the skin beneath.

"Soames!" she repeated, an accent almost of fear in her voice. "What do you mean about Soames?"

The inspector laughed, his keen little eyes watching every change in her face from beneath their lowered lids.

"Well, it is common knowledge—common gossip, perhaps I should say, that Mr. Soames is hoping to take a certain lady with him to the Daventry Arms when he goes there."

Pirnie recovered her self-possession with an effort.

"Hoping is one thing; doing is another. If Herbert Soames thinks that he can reckon on me and treat me as he likes—well, he will find out his mistake, that is all."

A faint smile gleamed for a second in the inspector's keen eyes. "Ay! When I saw you sitting here, I thought to myself that you might be waiting for Mr. Soames and hesitated about butting in. Then I thought again and I thought to myself, 'No, Miss Pirnie is the sort that men wait for, not that waits for them,' and came across to you. But if I have made a mistake—"

"You haven't!" Pirnie snapped. She got up with a jerk, her long black veil floating round her, the flush on her cheeks showing more plainly than ever against her rouge and powder. "Come, then, I believe I will go with you to the tea-rooms after all," she said, with an attempt at coquetry that deepened Furnival's unseen smile.

They walked across the Row, and went down the passage by the barracks. The tea-rooms were in a side street off Knightsbridge. Furnival was fortunate enough to secure a corner table and they sat down. He ordered a sumptuous tea. Pirnie's eyes sparkled. She loved the good things and bright places of life, and since Lady Anne's death she had felt as if she were living in some strange and horrible dream. She told herself now that surely this must be a very pleasant and unexpected awakening. Under the influence of the hot creamed tea and the hot buttered muffins she waxed loquacious, and, Furnival leading her on, chattered at considerable length about the household at Charlton Crescent. She little knew how much she revealed, but the precise information for which he was waiting did not come. He saw that he would have to put a few leading questions.

Hitching his chair a little nearer the table, he leaned across.

"I expect her ladyship did not often go out without you, Miss Pirnie?"

"Without me?" Pirnie opened her eyes. "Her ladyship hadn't been out without me for years. Even if Miss Fyvert or Miss Balmaine went with her, she would have me with her in case she wanted anything."

"Is that so? Well, I don't wonder at it," the inspector said gallantly. "But it is a funny thing now. A man I met the other day told me he saw Lady Anne Daventry driving up Piccadilly by herself one afternoon, it may be a month ago now."

Pirnie's eyes opened wider and wider. Her affectation dropped from her momentarily.

"That he never did, I will swear. Why, her ladyship hadn't been out for months before she died. Let me see—in October it would be—she went to buy a wedding present for Lord Fyvert, and when she came back home she said, 'Pirnie,' she said, 'it is the last time. It tires me too much. For the future the tradesmen will have to send their goods to me. I shall not go outside the garden.' And she kept to that, Mr. Furnival. Not once afterwards did she put her nose outside the garden."

"Um! That so?" said the inspector, stirring his tea thoughtfully. "Well, folks will say anything. Do you know what I heard the other day—that people are making bets that it was Lady Anne herself that sold her pearls and then pretended to have lost them!"

"What!" Genuine indignation coloured the maid's face now. "I never heard such a wicked thing in my life. My poor lady that never lived up to her income, and always put some by every year, to be accused of selling her own pearls that she loved so for the sake of her father and mother. Besides"—cooling down a little—"if she had done such a thing she would have kept quiet and nobody would have known anything about it in her lifetime. She would not have called the police in, it stands to reason, if she had sold them herself. Why should she?"

"Why, indeed?" The inspector gazed in front of him, pulling thoughtfully at his clean-shaven chin. "Besides, as you say, she couldn't have got to Spagnum's by herself and without your knowing."

"No, that she never did, I will swear," Pirnie answered positively.

"That settles the matter," the inspector said, taking up another cake and changing the subject. "You must be glad to get away from the house in Charlton Crescent, Miss Pirnie."

Pirnie clasped her hands. "Oh, I can't tell you how glad! It has been terrible there of late. Not knowing! And being afraid of everybody. Mr. Furnival—who do you think killed my lady?"

The inspector met the question with another. "Who do you?" he returned sharply.

Pirnie shivered. "I don't know," she whispered hoarsely. "But I am frightened—I dare not even think—"

The inspector reached over the tea-tray and laid his firm strong hand upon the quivering shaking one lying on the edge of the table. "Don't think of it," he advised. "Put it out of your mind. At any rate Lady Anne valued your services and appreciated them as you deserved. And you loved her—you had nothing to do with her awful fate. You could not help it."

To his consternation Pirnie burst into tears. "No! No! I could not help it," she sobbed. "I lie awake night after night thinking what I might have done to safeguard my lady."

"Shouldn't do that! It is very bad for you," the inspector said in a strictly non-committal voice.

There were not many people in the room, none really within earshot, but the few there were beginning to glance at them curiously. The inspector had no wish to be recognized.

"And now, dear lady, if you will put your handkerchief away and take another cup of tea, I will tell you a queer thing that has happened. It hasn't got into the papers yet, so far as I know."

Curiosity dried Pirnie's tears. "What is it, Mr. Furnival? You may depend upon me."

"I know I can," the inspector said with a sympathetic glance. "You would be a loyal friend, Miss Pirnie, whatever happened. And this is a terrible thing. The child has disappeared."

"The child!" Pirnie repeated in a tone only half comprehending and wholly incredulous. "You don't—you can't mean Miss Maureen?"

The inspector nodded. "Yes! She disappeared while travelling down to North Coton yesterday with the Fyverts and her sister and Miss Balmaine."

"Disappeared!" Pirnie's eyes grew round with horror. "Inspector, how could she—out of a railway carriage?"

The inspector coughed. "Well, I didn't mean literally out of a railway carriage. As a matter of fact she was seen at the junction. Every one seems to have thought she was with some one else and she was not discovered to be missing until they reached North Coton Rectory. Her sister is nearly out of her mind."

"Poor Miss Dorothy! So I should think!" Pirnie sat silent a minute, her eyes looking straight before her. The inspector watched her keenly between his mouthfuls of buttered muffin.

"Mr. Furnival, this can't have had anything to do with my lady's death—Miss Maureen can't know anything! It is an impossibility!"

The inspector finished his muffin and took a long draught of tea before answering. Then his cup was pushed away from him.

"Miss Pirnie, I may trust you with what wouldn't tell another person living. I'll be hanged if can make out whether she does or she doesn't. There has always to my mind been something queer about the child. But I can't see how she could have been connected with the murder and that is a fact! Still, it seems to me that someone must have had a motive for getting her away. What do you think of this Alice Gray that she was so friendly with?"

Pirnie tossed her head. "I never was one to take up with the under servants. Alice knew her work and her place, and did the one and kept the other. That was all I knew about her. When she was set to wait on Miss Maureen because the child could not go to school and took a fancy to her, I thought it was a good thing. For Miss Maureen was a handful! But there, Alice could not have run away with her!"

"Of course she couldn't," the inspector assented. But his tone was neither convincing nor convinced.

"Anyhow, Alice Gray gave the police her home address, somewhere out past New Barnet. She said she was going there at once, and in fact was seen off on her way by the footman. But she never arrived there. At least she hadn't last night."

"Well, I never!" Words failed the maid for a minute. "We are living in queer times, Mr. Furnival," she said at last. "I often wish my lot had been cast in the good old days when folks could at least sleep in their beds at night in peace."

"The world would have been a good deal poorer to-day if your wish had been granted, Miss Pirnie," the inspector said gallantly. "But now, I have upset you, and it is vexing me past a bit. You will be losing your good looks and that would be more than I could stand. Miss Maureen and Alice Gray will be found very soon, both of them, you may take it from me. And, look here, how would it be if I was to look in at your place sometime this week of an evening? I might have some news for you—that would set your mind at rest."

Pirnie stood up and adjusted her hat and drew on her long gauntlet gloves. "That would be very kind of you," she said unsteadily. "But—I don't know. Perhaps it would be better not, inspector. I expect I shall hear if there is any good news to hear soon—somehow."

"Perhaps it might upset some one else if I called?" suggested the inspector. "Maybe, Mr. Soames—"

The woman's half-averted face turned crimson. "Please do not speak of Mr. Soames. He is nothing to me."

"That so?" the inspector said in a satisfied tone. "Then there is nothing to prevent you and me from being friends, is there, Miss Pirnie? I shall do myself the pleasure of calling in, maybe to-morrow evening, and bringing you any news there may be."

"I should be glad to hear about Miss Maureen," Pirnie said primly, but her eyes looked well pleased as they glanced at the inspector's meagre, lithe form.

They turned out of the restaurant together and made their way back to the roar of the traffic in Knightsbridge. There Pirnie stopped.

"I get my bus just here, Mr. Furnival, so I will say good-bye, and thank you very much," holding out her hand.

The inspector pressed it tenderly.

"I shall only say au revoir. Oh, one moment more. There is one thing you might tell me and save me a letter to Mr. Soames, if you would be so kind, Miss Pirnie. There is a quantity of clothing—men's clothing—in a bedroom on the third floor. It isn't Mr. John Daventry's—it isn't big enough. I don't suppose for a moment it has any bearing on the case, but it is my duty just to ascertain to whom it belongs."

"Oh, you mean packed away in the lumber room?" Pirnie said as he stopped. "They belonged to Mr. Frank—her ladyship's son, the youngest, that was killed in the war. Her ladyship used to talk sometimes of giving them away—but she could never bring herself to do so."

"Oh, daresay not!" But the inspector's tone was abstracted. His eyes were smiling into Pirnie's as he helped her into a bus, his hand held hers closely, and when he stood back to let other passengers get in he still watched her and remained watching until the bus was out of sight. It was little wonder that Pirnie's maiden heart was fluttering as she made her way to her suburban home.

The inspector walked back across the park. There were heavy furrows across his brow. His keen gimlet eyes glanced unseeingly at the faces of the few riders left in the Row. It was evident that his thoughts were far away. It would have been evident to those who knew the Ferret best that his mind was busy with some knotty problem—that in some way he had been surprised, probably unexpectedly puzzled.

As he emerged into Bayswater Road near the Lancaster Gate tube, he glanced at the news posters of the men outside the station. "The house in Charlton Crescent," he read. "Curious development."

He scowled at the unlucky vendor as he took a copy of the paper. As he feared, Maureen's disappearance had somehow become public, though not all the circumstances. But there was a description of the missing child.

The inspector's scowl deepened as thrusting the offending paper deep down in his pocket he set off at a brisk pace for Charlton Crescent.

As he entered the Crescent the door of Lady Anne's house was thrown open and Dorothy Fyvert appeared on the steps with Bruce Cardyn close behind.

It was evident that she had been crying. Her eyes were red-rimmed, her lips were trembling. She caught the inspector's arm.

"We have had a message," she cried breathlessly. "Alice has come home alone and denies all knowledge of Maureen. Oh, inspector, what has become of my little sister?"

"Heaven knows!" said the inspector heavily.

CHAPTER XVI

"AND NOW WHAT does Alice Gray say she has been doing?"

Inspector Furnival was the speaker. He had drawn Miss Fyvert and Bruce Cardyn back into the hall.

"Your message came from Cuthbertson, suppose?" He spoke rapidly over his shoulder to Bruce Cardyn, while Dorothy clung to his hands as though she derived some subtle comfort from their warm human contact.

"Cuthbertson," Cardyn assented. "I wired back for particulars. The answer came just now. Gray got out of the train at Golders Green and took a bus back to Victoria. Went to Brighton to see her cousin. Address given—I am verifying."

At this moment there was an interruption. A car stopped before the door and a man sprang out, took the steps in his stride, and hammered at the door.

Cardyn opened it. "Mr. Daventry!"

"Yes, Mr. Daventry!" that individual assented, flinging his hat and motor-goggles on the old oak table and throwing his heavy fur-lined coat on one of the big chairs. "Now, Dorothy, what is this I hear? What have you been doing with Maureen?"

"Oh, John! We can't think what has become of her. If we don't find her I shall go mad."

"Oh, we shall find her safe enough," returned John Daventry in the loud cheerful voice that never seemed to admit of failure. "What—what's this, Dorothy? Crying? Oh, come, I can't have that. Maureen will turn up right enough, little monkey! Oh, I see Mr. Detective Furnival can't find her! Well, you know, he hasn't found the bally blighter who got up to the window and killed Aunt Anne. But I am going to look for Maureen myself."

The inspector smiled faintly. His eyes watched the young man's pleasant face with its bronzed ruddy skin, clear blue eyes and the white teeth that spoke of perfect health. Eminently a clean, wholesome, desirable-looking young Englishman, but hardly the material of which a successful sleuth is made.

"I am sure I hope you will find her, Mr. Daventry," he returned politely. "It is not always so easy to discover things, you know."

"Well, I ought to, seeing how often you fail," retorted Daventry with a grin. "See here, there's that damned Cat Burglar, you can't find him. You don't know who stabbed Aunt Anne or who stole her pearls. And now you can't find Maureen. One, two, three, four failures! You will have to take care it does not become a habit, Furnival!"

The inspector did not look quite pleased as he turned away.

Daventry glanced at Dorothy.

"I shall go to Alice's home at New Barnet myself. I'll make her tell me what has become of Maureen, or I will know the reason why."

"If she knows," Dorothy said with a catch in her breath. "But suppose she does not? Oh, John, I fancy all sorts of things. It will drive me mad if all this uncertainty goes on. Oh, when I think of the horrible cruelties that are inflicted upon children—sometimes I ask myself, if it is possible that some villain has got hold of Maureen—"

She stopped abruptly, but her big eyes as she gazed imploringly at her cousin held an evergrowing haunting horror.

"No!" thundered Daventry. "Of course it is not possible! Maureen is safe enough, only up to mischief, expect. Why, Dorothy, what puts such horrible thoughts into your head? Don't let yourself even think of such terrible things. Put them out of your mind."

"If I can," Dorothy said, her voice dropping to the merest whisper. "But I can't, John. I am haunted—haunted by the fear—the horror of what may have become of her."

"I will find her for you," Daventry promised, touching her hand lightly. "I am going to motor straight off to Alice. And I will wring the truth out of her—I will bring Maureen back."

He stopped as there was another knock at the door. Dorothy looked vaguely comforted. There was something so reassuring about John Daventry's power and certainty, that she began to believe that he would succeed where the detectives had failed.

Daventry and she had been friends from their earliest years, until the friendship under the pressure of their two families had merged into the sort of indefinable understanding which to both had become irksome, and to Dorothy, of late, intolerable. But to-day, looking at the firm, strong mouth, at the clear, straight eyes, some of Dorothy's old confidence returned. She tried to smile at him.

"I am sure you will if anybody can, John."

"That I will!" he said, looking her squarely in the eyes. "There will be no beating about the bush with the Cat Burglar with me, I promise you!" He stopped short. "What is that?"

The inspector opened the front door, though none of the others had heard either bell or knocker. Now he seemed to be carrying on a colloquy with some one outside.

As John Daventry listened his face changed; the steel-grey eyes grew softer, the rather hard mouth softened and grew tender.

The voice speaking to the inspector became more distinct. "It was the only thing I could do, inspector, to bring her to you. Now, Susan, do not be so foolish! You have nothing to be afraid of if you speak the truth."

It was Margaret Balmaine speaking. Daventry hurried to the door just as she entered holding a shivering, weeping figure by the arm. The inspector followed them and closed the door.

Dorothy uttered a cry of surprise as she recognized the maid whom she and Margaret shared.

"Why, Susan, what in the world is the matter? Are you ill?"

"No, she is not ill. She is frightened," Margaret Balmaine answered for her. Miss Balmaine herself was looking curiously shaken out of her usual composure. In spite of her "make-up" it was quite evident that her face was very white. Her big, artificially-darkened eyes were filled with dread. Yet she kept her hold on the arm of the weeping girl by her side.

"Now, Susan, speak up! I promise you nothing will happen to you if you tell what you know. Come, dry your eyes and speak out."

Thus adjured, the girl made a desperate attempt to obey.

"It was what I heard them say," she said, between her sobs. "I couldn't help it—I wasn't listening."

"No, no! We know that—none of us think you were," Margaret Balmaine assured her. "Come, Susan, where were you? Just repeat what you told me a minute ago."

The inspector watched both girls closely. Not a movement of either escaped him, but for once the keen ferret eyes looked puzzled, one might almost have said bewildered. Miss Balmaine touched the girl's arm again encouragingly.

"Come, Susan!"

At last the girl's sobs stopped. She rolled her wet handkerchief up into a crumpled ball, and held it in her hot little hand.

"I was sitting doing some needlework in Miss Fyvert's room," she began, speaking in a controlled almost mechanical voice, "and Miss Maureen was ill—stopping in her room, which opened out of Miss Dorothy's. She did not know I was there, for I heard her moving about, opening and shutting drawers. And if she had known I was there she would have spoken, for Miss Maureen was never one to keep quiet. didn't want her just then, either, so I kept quiet too, and was just going to slip out of the room when I heard Alice begin to speak. 'It's no good, Maureen,' she began—and that surprised me, to hear her speak without the "Miss"—'I mean, that man has been asking questions again. He will find out everything and then what will become of us?' I ought to have come away, I know," Susan's voice became choked with sobs again. She dabbed her hard little handkerchief in her eyes. "Or else have spoken out, but I was wondering what they meant, and I stayed and have been sorry ever since."

Dorothy sprang forward impatiently. "Oh, never mind about that. What did you hear? Hurry, hurry, girl, for Heaven's sake!"

Susan's sobs redoubled. "I'm being as quick as I can, Miss Dorothy. It isn't so very easy," she said thickly. "When Alice said: 'What will become of us?' Miss Maureen began to cry. 'Can they send us to prison, Alice?' she says, crying all the time like. Alice, she began to cry too. 'I am sure they can,' she sobs. 'The thing that I am afraid of is that they will—leastways they won't you, because you are too young, but they will maybe hang me, and that will kill my mother. Oh, dear; oh, dear! what shall I do?' And she begins to sob again. With that Miss Maureen gives a sharp cry. 'Oh, Alice! Alice! They—they mustn't hang us—nor put us in prison. If only we could get away, where that horrid, horrid inspector man could not find us!'"

Susan said the last sentence with a certain zeal that sounded as if she relished repeating the obnoxious adjectives to the inspector's face.

"Well! Go on!" John Daventry's voice was harsh and strained. "What else did you hear?" Susan turned to him with an odd little bow.

"That was all, Mr. Daventry, sir. Miss Fyvert went into the room. I heard her speak to Alice about some needlework and slipped away. I don't know what they were talking about. I couldn't think. But I didn't bother so much about it until we heard yesterday that Miss Maureen had disappeared. Then—then I got frightened and Miss Balmaine made me tell her—"

"Yes," said Margaret Balmaine in a cold, determined voice. "I found Susan crying and could get no explanation at first except that she was frightened and wanted to leave. At that suspected that she must know something. I taxed her with it and after some time she told me this. Naturally I could not deal with it myself, so thought the best thing was to bring her round to you, inspector. I don't know whether what she knows is any help, whether it may have bearing on the case, I mean. But it seemed to me you ought to know."

It struck Bruce Cardyn, looking at him, that the Ferret had a baffled, puzzled expression absolutely foreign to his keen little face.

"Quite right, Miss Balmaine," he said politely. "I wish everyone would be as prompt and sensible. Now, my girl"—turning to Susan—"there is nothing for you to cry about, if you have told us the whole truth. That was all you heard?"

"Every word, sir," corroborated the weeping Susan.

The inspector opened the door. "Then there is no great purpose to be served by keeping you. Try to put it out of your mind for the time being. And above all things do not cry about it."

Susan needed no second bidding. She slipped out of the opened door with one of those queer, semi-circular little bows of hers, and made off down the Crescent as fast as her legs could carry her.

The group of men and women standing in the hall looked at one another in horrified consternation. At last Dorothy spoke:

"What does it mean? Maureen couldn't have known—couldn't have done anything—about Aunt Anne!"

"Of course she couldn't!" John Daventry said roughly. "Don't be a fool, Dorothy! Poor little Maureen. The child must have been scared out of her senses. That is what it means."

But though his tone was decided, his voice gruff almost to bearishness, his face had turned again that sickly greenish colour, his grey eyes evaded both the girls. It was curious, too, that the same tint seemed to have spread from him to Bruce Cardyn, that even the inspector's usually ruddy colour had faded to a dull grey hue.

Neither Dorothy nor Margaret could well have been paler. The silence lasted a minute longer. Then it was broken in an odd way. Margaret Balmaine laughed aloud, a harsh, grating sound that broke in her throat in a high choking laugh.

"Fancy Maureen killing Aunt Anne!" she cried, between her spasms. "Just fancy Maureen or even Alice killing Aunt Anne!"

CHAPTER XVII

"No NEWS?" questioned the inspector as Bruce Cardyn hung the receiver up and turned from the telephone with an exclamation of impatience.

"No news!" he assented. "Sometimes I think there never will be."

The inspector's little ferret-like eyes glanced at him keenly for a moment, then turned back to a parcel he was slowly unfolding.

"Give us time!" he remarked philosophically. "We shall find it all out some day. But it is not so easy to put one of those things—jig-saw puzzles—together, if all the important pieces are in the hands of different people who refuse to give them up. This case reminds me of that."

"Why?" Cardyn inquired laconically.

"Because nobody—I say nobody, advisedly—will speak the truth about his or her little bit of the puzzle. Now you have your own little corner which you are trying to get straight. That little piece of the corner on which you are busy probably dovetails into some other bit and the two joined together might make a whole large piece of the puzzle plain. When are you going to speak out, Mr. Cardyn?"

For a moment Cardyn stared at him in amazement, then a glance of comprehension flashed into his grey eyes.

"You shall be the first to hear when I know anything definite, inspector. At present it is only vague surmise and suspicions that are probably unjustifiable."

"Nevertheless," said the inspector firmly, "I think we will have the surmises and the suspicions out in the open, if you please."

Bruce met his penetrating gaze squarely. "Will you give me an hour or two? I think—I hope that by then I may have something definite to tell you."

The inspector nodded. "Wait till to-night," he said gruffly. "And now look at these!"

Bruce glanced at the white plaster of Paris objects that were gradually emerging from their wrappings under Inspector Furnival's capable fingers.

"Footprints! Those in the border under the window in the hall?" he questioned.

Inspector Furnival touched them gingerly with the tip of his finger.

"Ay! Beautifully done, aren't they? You can't beat my man, Botts, at this sort of thing. Now, what do you make of this, Mr. Cardyn?"

Bruce Cardyn bent over them. "Small size—eights, I should say."

"Right! No, Mr. Cardyn, what do you make of them?"

"That the murderer was a man with small feet."

"If he wore them," the inspector said significantly.

Cardyn looked at him. "Who else would be likely to?"

"That is what we are trying to find out," the inspector said sapiently.

"You mean?"

"Perhaps we shall each find out what the other means later on," the inspector said dryly. "In the meantime may I remind you that there were three men among the persons in the fatal room. Two of them Mr. John Daventry and Soames, take the same size of shoe—ten. The third—yourself—"

"I take nines," Cardyn said quietly. "Though I daresay I might get into eights. All my shoes are at your disposal. Those in my rooms as well as the few pairs have here. Probably, however, you know all that is to be known about them already."

A slight spasm—was it a smile?—momentarily contracted Inspector Furnival's sharp-featured little face.

"Mr. Cardyn, I am going to show you a pair of shoes that exactly fit those footprints." He led the way across the hall and up the staircase. Past the death chamber on the first floor, past Lady Anne's bedroom, past those belonging to the two girls, past the one Bruce had occupied, right up to the servants' quarters on the top floor went he. Then he unlocked a door Bruce had not seen open before.

"The lumber-room," he said briefly. "Always kept locked in Lady Anne's time."

It was a small room. The houses in Charlton Crescent were not big enough to have much space for lumber-rooms, and it was almost entirely filled with boxes.

"All locked!" the inspector said, waving his hand comprehensively around. "Lady Anne believed in safeguarding her property and her life. It is the very irony of fate."

As he spoke he was unfastening a huge wooden chest that stood under the window. Inside there appeared to be an unusual and incongruous collection of things, arranged in no particular order. Articles of clothing were mingled with books and papers. One corner was entirely given up to shoes. The inspector put his footprints down carefully on another box and chose out a pair of shoes. Then placing them beside the plaster of Paris models, he pointed to Cardyn. "The shoes that made those prints. See for yourself!"

Bruce compared the two point by point. They fitted exactly. Even the place where the heel was a little worn down had its counterpart in the cast. He looked at the inspector.

"No doubt about that! You have the originals safe enough? But how did they come there?"

"That," said the inspector slowly, "I should very much like to discover. You know to whom this chest and its contents belonged, perhaps?"

Bruce shook his head. "I have not the least idea."

"To Frank Daventry—Lady Anne's youngest son," the inspector said impressively. "When he went out to France he left a lot of things here. After his death most of them were packed up and brought here by Lady Anne's orders."

"But how—" Bruce Cardyn looked like a man thoroughly dazed.

"Ah, how!" the inspector echoed. "Another little piece of the jig-saw puzzle, Mr. Cardyn. A regular bit of snag too, for you think that pair of shoes just like the others I suppose?"

Cardyn scrutinized them all round; then he picked up one of the pair in question and compared it silently with several of the others. At last he looked up.

"This boot is a little wider than the others. I should say they were eights with a five fitting. Probably this is an eight with a six fitting."

"Right!" the inspector said laconically. "Well?"

"I never knew a fellow alter the size of his boots unless he had an attack of gout—or something of that sort," Cardyn observed.

"No." Inspector Furnival put the two of them together. "If you look you will find that every shoe in that box is made by the same shoemaker—except this pair that fit the footprints. They have inside the name of a well-known firm of American bootmakers in the Strand-—John D. Palmer and Co. Now I paid Mr. John D. Palmer a visit the other day and made a few inquiries. As a result discovered that this particular shoe, though to the lay mind it looks very much like any other, has been on the market only about twelve months, which naturally precludes the idea of their having any connexion with Frank Daventry."

Bruce Cardyn paled, detective though he was. In that moment he seemed to realize something of the tortuous, devilish mind they were up against.

"They must have been put here by the murderer," he said.

"Not necessarily. One must look at the thing all round. Some one may have found them and put them here to shield the real criminal."

Bruce Cardyn did not look convinced. He had taken up the shoes once more and was examining them with meticulous care, and comparing them point by point with the plaster of Paris models. The inspector's keen little eyes followed every movement. At last Cardyn looked up.

"The impression is much deeper at the toes than at the heels. It looks to me as if the murderer had sprung out backwards, standing on his toes while he shut the window behind him, and—"

"Yes! And?" The inspector prompted gently as the younger paused with a bewildered expression. "The footprints went no farther."

"I know," Bruce assented. "But how the beggar got off has always been a puzzle to me. Sometimes I have thought that he put down stones and sprang from one to the other, pulling up the last one as he took another step."

"Ingenious," said the inspector, "but it won't wash. In the first place he would have had a large stone on which to balance himself if he pulled the back one up. In the second, look at the time he would have wasted, with innumerable opportunities of detection. Thirdly, why should he take so much trouble to avoid the soil of the border, when he had already left two well-defined foot-prints in the most conspicuous place, right under the window?"

He waited for a reply, but none came. Bruce Cardyn was still examining the shoes, his brows drawn together in a frown.

The inspector pointed to the toes again. "Curiously deep impression the toes have made, haven't they?"

"I don't know that it is any deeper than one would expect if a man sprang from the window on to some soil that had been freshly dug."

The inspector rapped the cast with his pencil. "A man springs down upon his toes—granted—but then he lets himself down upon his heels—he doesn't remain standing on his toes. Now the impressions of the heels are of the slightest. The wearer of these shoes neither stood firmly on his feet nor turned."

"You mean," said Cardyn slowly, "that the—the person who wore those shoes jumped on to the border purposely to make those impressions, and then got back into the house, wishing to give the impression that the murderer had left that way."

"Precisely," said the inspector dryly. "I couldn't have put the case better myself if I had been laying it before the chief himself."

"The inference being," Bruce went on, his voice controlled as ever, though a very dangerous look was growing in his eyes, "that the shoes were worn by someone in the house. Further that as I was the only one of the three men who could by any possibility get into the shoes—I must be the assassin, Inspector Furnival."

The inspector held up his hand.

"Steady, please. You are taking a little bit too much for granted, Mr. Cardyn. Though those are a man's shoes, that does not prove that a man wore them when the footprints were made."

"You cannot mean that one of the girls—" Bruce uttered.

"It might have been or might not," the inspector said with judicial calm. "There is nothing inherently impossible in the idea, as I hope to presently show you. A woman might perfectly easily have made the footprints either definitely to turn suspicion from herself or her lover. Now to come back to business. After an enormous amount of trouble I have managed to get something from the shop where these were sold—a list of the names on the books. It is not complete, of course, and quite inconclusive since many people pay ready money for their shoes. But there was one name on their books and only one that was familiar to me in this case."

The inspector was not often guilty of pausing for effect, but his hesitation was now dramatic.

No shade of enlightenment came into Cardyn's eyes as far as the inspector could see.

"What name?" he questioned breathlessly.

"The name," said Inspector Furnival watching the effect of each word as it dropped from his lips, "was that of your predecessor—David Branksome!"

CHAPTER XVIII

"Twenty-five Todmorden Lane, Ryston, N."

Even with his extensive knowledge of London and its suburbs the above address had puzzled Inspector Furnival. At last, however, he had found Todmorden Lane, tucked away between two of the better-known streets. Just as he turned into it a car stopped behind him and a familiar voice exclaimed:

"Why, Inspector Furnival, I declare! On the same errand as myself, I dare bet!"

The inspector did not look too pleased.

"I thought you were here yesterday, Mr. Daventry."

"So I was," John Daventry returned, with a scowl that sat ill upon his pleasant, open face. "But Alice was out—slipped out by the back door as I came up to the front, expect."

"Ah, well, she won't do that to-day—not unseen, anyway," the inspector said grimly. "My man— Cuthbertson—is watching the house."

"Pity he wasn't yesterday," John Daventry growled.

"I expect he was," the inspector said placidly. "Probably when she went out of the back door he shadowed her. To-day, however, if she is not at home we shall soon find her."

Number twenty-five was not the cleanest of the houses in Todmorden Lane; there were the usual Nottingham lace curtains over the front window, drawn back to show the aspidistra between, but the steps and the door-knocker looked neglected, the dingy curtains could not disguise the dirtiness of the windows.

Mr. Daventry seized the knocker and banged it loudly.

"If you wished to frighten our prey," the inspector said mildly, "you could hardly go a better way to do it."

"I do mean to frighten the truth out of her," John Daventry muttered between his teeth.

"It isn't always the truth you frighten out of people," the inspector said wisely.

John Daventry did not answer. His knock at the door had brought a speedy response.

In curious contrast with John Daventry's vigorous assault upon it, the door was opened just a little way slowly and very noiselessly, and a woman looked out—a little drab-coloured woman with hair already going grey, though she was only old with that pathetic early age of the hardworked and the very poor.

As she saw John Daventry who stood well in front of the inspector she uttered a low cry. "Oh dear! Oh dear!" She tried to close the door again but Daventry had got his foot inside.

"Now, Mrs. Gray, is that daughter of yours at home to-day?"

The woman shrank back and, realizing the uselessness of resistance let the door slip from her grasp. "Oh dear! Oh dear!"

"Is she at home, I ask?" pursued John Daventry, pushing his foot forward until he could insert his knee and push the door and Mrs. Gray back together.

Mrs. Gray threw her apron over her face and began to weep noisily. The inspector followed Daventry into the narrow entry, called by courtesy a hall, as Mrs. Gray fell back against the wall.

"Leave this to me, Mr. Daventry," he said authoritatively. "Mrs. Gray, your daughter has nothing to fear from us if she will just answer a few questions quietly."

"She don't know nothing of what Miss Maureen done," wailed Mrs. Gray inconsequently.

"Well, she has only to tell us so," the inspector said politely. "Ah, there you are!" as through a half-open door on the right he caught sight of a tall white-faced girl supporting herself by her hand against the table. "Now, now, don't alarm yourself"— as the girl began to shake visibly and to look on the verge of collapse—"we just want to know what you did at Brighton the other day."

"Nothing—I didn't do anything!" the girl muttered sullenly. But though she answered Furnival it was at Daventry she was glancing with frightened eyes. What importance had any policeman in the world to her compared with Mr. Daventry?

John Daventry answered the glance.

"Tell us where Maureen is," he said thickly. "We know that you took her to Brighton with you. You have both been traced there; where is she now?"

The girl threw out her hands. "I don't know, I wish to Heaven I did!"

She flung herself down on a wooden chair beside her and burst into loud suffocating sobs. The anger in John Daventry's usually good-tempered face deepened.

"What have you done with her?" he demanded. "Where is she now? When did you leave her? Speak the truth now or by the Lord in Heaven I will wring your blasted neck for you!"

He seemed to have forgotten Furnival's presence, and that functionary elected to remain an inactive spectator, though to those who knew the Ferret it would have been obvious that eyes and ears were alike vigilantly on the alert.

"I don't—know," she said, the words coming out between bursts of sobbing. "I couldn't tell you any more, sir, not if you was to murder me, and—and I shouldn't mind if you did!"

John Daventry glared at her. Assuredly, had she been a man, he would have been as good as his word. He would have taken her by the throat and shaken the truth out of her.

As it was, standing over her, he looked so big and strong, so thoroughly capable of carrying out his threat, that he literally frightened her into speech.

"Where did you last see her?" he thundered.

Alice lifted her tear-stained face. "On the front at Brighton, sir. I only took my eyes off her one minute, and the next she was gone. I searched for her everywhere for hours, but not a trace of her could I find. That is God's truth, Mr. Daventry, sir. And I couldn't tell you any more—not if you were to hang me for it."

John Daventry stared at her. "Do you mean to say—"

Inspector Furnival put him quietly aside. "No one is likely to hang you, my good girl, or to try to punish you in any way. We only want to find the child for her sister's sake. She said 'Alice will tell you all she knows if you say how anxious I am! I always liked Alice—she was a good girl—and I think she liked me,'" finished the inspector, improvising as he went on.

"Which I always did," Alice sobbed. "We all did. And I would never have taken Miss Maureen to Brighton, if I had thought of such a thing happening. But Miss Maureen, she had set her heart on going and she gave me no peace."

"I see." The inspector's voice grew gentle. "We quite realize that you are not to blame. But, now, will you tell me just what happened? Begin at the very beginning."

John Daventry opened his mouth as though he were going to intervene at this juncture, but a warning gesture from the inspector checked him and he remained with his mouth slightly open, staring at them.

"I—I met Miss Maureen at the junction," said Alice, beginning to speak a little more clearly. "And—and we went back to town and then changed to Victoria and came to Brighton. My cousin had some rooms to let and we meant to stay there for a time. But we put our luggage in the cloak-room and went for a walk along the front first. Miss Maureen was that pleased to get away from—from the house in Charlton Crescent that she was dancing about all excited like. But I was tired, we had had to do a lot before we left, but speak to Miss Maureen as I might she wouldn't be quiet. There were some children dancing about to an organ that an old woman was playing and Miss Maureen went and danced with them. I asked her not to go, but it was no good."

John Daventry nodded his head. He knew Maureen only too well in this mood and quite realized that Alice could have had no easy task.

"I think—I think I must have dozed a minute," the girl went on. "I had been up early in the morning and was tired, but it was only a minute. Miss Maureen was then jumping about like anything when I closed my eyes. When I opened them again not a bit of her could I see. They told me afterwards that I rushed about like a wild woman. The old woman was still there with her organ, and the children were dancing about. There didn't seem to be any difference except that Miss Maureen was not there."

"What happened next?" the inspector questioned in that new tonelessly gentle voice of his. "What did you do?"

"Do!" Alice Gray echoed. "I ran up and down Brighton streets looking here, there and everywhere I thought the child might have got to. I just ran till I was ready to drop, and then went to my cousin's. There didn't seem anything else to be done."

"It did not strike you that the proper thing to do was to go to the police station and report the child's disappearance?" the inspector said quietly.

Alice stared at him. "No! No! I couldn't do that," she wailed. "I couldn't do anything. I just came home and waited."

"If you had gone to the police they would have probably found her in half an hour," said the inspector quietly. "Now, however, it is no use crying over spilt milk."

"Do you mean that there is no more to be done?" John Daventry demanded.

The inspector shrugged his shoulders.

"Not at present, I'm afraid."

Daventry made no rejoinder, but his frown was ominous. Alice looked relieved. The inspector's eyes did not miss one shade of her expression.

"There is nothing to be done but to set all the resources of Scotland Yard to work to find the child." He turned to John Daventry and said a few words in an undertone. Then he looked back at Alice.

"Why did you take the child to Brighton?" he asked sharply. "Why did you want to hide yourselves?"

Alice's hands dropped on her lap. Every vestige of colour faded from her face. In the silence that followed you could fancy you could hear her heart beating.

"Hide ourselves!" she breathed at last. "We—we didn't want to hide ourselves. Miss—Miss Maureen wanted to see Brighton."

"Stop!" The inspector's tones had altered to sternness. "We know that you were frightened, that you were both frightened, that there was something in connexion with Lady Anne's—death! Ah!"

He sprang forward as he spoke and caught the girl just as she reeled off the chair in a dead faint.

The inspector laid her on the rough couch at the end of the window. Then glancing round the room he caught up a glass of water and dashed it into the girl's face. It had the instant effect of bringing back her senses. She sat up and brushed back the wet hair from her face.

"You said that if I told you about Miss Maureen that was all—all!" she murmured.

"If you told me the whole truth," the inspector said significantly. "Think again, my girl. The whole truth if you please."

But Alice was lying back in her chair ready to faint again. "The truth! the truth!" she murmured. "I have told you the truth."

"The whole truth," the inspector corrected.

Alice scarcely seemed to hear him. She was murmuring: "The truth! the truth!" to herself.

The inspector shrugged his shoulders as he glanced across at John Daventry. "We shall do no more good here to-day, Mr. Daventry. It is sheer waste of time."

John Daventry muttered a sulky assent, and the two men turned away. At the front door which Mrs. Gray was still holding open in a dreary, senseless fashion, the inspector waited to allow John Daventry to precede him. Then with a muttered word of apology he returned swiftly to the kitchen.

Alice sat up with a startled cry as he stepped quickly to her side.

"When you are thinking over what you will say to me, the next time—don't forget the connexion with the Cat Burglar," he said suggestively.

Then he turned away from her as quickly as he had come in. As he did so he cannoned into John Daventry who had followed him. But the inspector did not stop. With another apology he hurried out of the house.

With his quick stride John Daventry caught him up on the narrow pavement outside. "I heard you!" he said hoarsely. "I heard you just now."

In one swift glance the inspector saw that the ruddy colour had faded from the young man's face—that beneath its tan it had turned grey and cold.

"Heard me just now?" he questioned blandly.

"Yes! Heard you!" John Daventry repeated. "What did you mean? You asked about the Cat Burglar."

The inspector turned and looked him full in the face, an odd expression gleaming for a moment in the sharp little eyes.

"What does she know about the Cat Burglar?" he repeated. "Well, I am inclined to think that she knows more about the Cat Burglar than anyone, Mr. Daventry."

"But—but—" John Daventry's utterance became choked. The big veins in his forehead stood out like whipcord. His face swelled, but he did not turn red, instead its sickly grey tint became more pronounced against the tan of his skin. He put up one big hand and wrenched at his collar as though he were stifling.

"But—but—" he gasped incoherently. "If—if you know that she knows all about the Cat Burglar—then you must know about him too."

The inspector raised his eyebrows. "Not necessarily! But—supposing that I do know something. Have you never had any suspicion, Mr. Daventry?"

"Never, so help me Heaven!" John Daventry asseverated thickly.

CHAPTER XIX

"No news?"

Bruce Cardyn shook his head. "Not so far. The inspector may be back any moment."

"He would have phoned through if he had had any good news," Dorothy Fyvert said miserably. "And if he cannot make Alice speak no one can."

"Mr. John Daventry may possibly," Cardyn suggested.

"He won't," Dorothy said in a mildly contemptuous voice. "John will bluster and rage, but he will never get the truth out of Alice."

"Suppose the truth has already been told?" Bruce Cardyn suggested. He was looking grave and tired. His eyes were red-rimmed and had an extinguished look—the sort of look that comes to a man who has been sitting up several nights in succession. Lady Anne Daventry's death was taking heavy toll of those who were engaged in trying to probe the secret of it.

Dorothy herself was looking wretchedly ill. This terrible anxiety about Maureen coming on the top of the horror of her aunt's death had turned the bright healthy girl who came home with the Barminsters to the house in Charlton Crescent into a mere nervous wreck. She had not been to bed, she had not taken off her clothes since she heard that her sister was missing, and she spent her whole time walking, backwards and forwards, up and down the streets. She firmly believed that Maureen would come or be brought to her in those same streets. Sometimes Margaret Balmaine was with her—sometimes Susan. More often she was alone.

It went to the heart of the man who loved her to see her as she was now. Her bright fair hair looked disordered and dull under a hat thrust on anyhow. Her brown eyes were bloodshot from much weeping and had great dark half-circles beneath them. The clear tones of her complexion were blurred and her face itself looked sodden and swollen. Her usually soft red lips were cracked and discoloured and every now and then they twitched uncontrollably. But Dorothy cared nothing about her appearance. She could think of nothing but Maureen—Maureen whom her imagination pictured in more and more terrible straits as the hours went on.

She had just paused in her endless pacing of the streets to call at the house in Charlton Crescent to see whether there was any news of Maureen.

It was the day of the inspector and John Daventry's visit to Todmorden Lane, and Bruce Cardyn was at Lady Anne's house to meet the inspector.

"How do you mean—that Alice has told the truth?" Dorothy questioned feverishly.

"Well, I am inclined to think that, when she says she does not know where the child is, she is speaking the truth," he said slowly.

"But if she does not, where on earth can Maureen be?"

"I don't know," Bruce said in a strangely abstracted tone. "But we are bound to know soon," he added.

He was still holding the door open. Dorothy had come into the hall and was standing with her back to it. He watched the outgoings and the incomings in the Crescent with the same abstracted look. A motor came whizzing up to the next door. For a moment Bruce thought that one of the two men in it was the inspector, then he saw that both were strangers. An organ-grinder was playing a melancholy ditty outside the Crescent; a little beggar boy came round from the other side and sat down on the first doorstep, leaning his head against the doorpost.

"I don't know that we are bound to know soon," Dorothy contradicted. "I heard the other day—somebody told me in a shop where I was making inquiries—that a mother sent her child to school as usual one day in a little country town. She stood on the doorstep to watch her as far as she could. It was only a little way to the school, such a very little way that there was only one field with a footpath running right through it that was really out of the mother's sight until the child came out in the village street. The child turned to wave her hand to her mother before she went through the handgate, and from that day to this neither word nor sign has come from her. She disappeared as completely and utterly as though the earth had swallowed her up. The villagers went out in bands to search for her. Scotland Yard sent down detectives and of course the local police were very busy from the first, but not the smallest trace of her could any of them discover—or has ever been discovered. Mr. Cardyn, do you wonder that the poor mother went mad—that to this day she is confined in a lunatic asylum and that she spends all her days in trying to find something? She does not know what, fortunately. The memory of her little child has a good deal faded, only she knows that it is a very precious thing that she looks for constantly. Mr. Cardyn, suppose we never find Maureen—we never know what has become of her?" And Dorothy shook from head to foot as she spoke.

"I refuse to imagine anything so appalling," Bruce Cardyn said at once.

But it seemed to Dorothy Fyvert that his manner had altered—that some assurance had gone from him, that he was trying to evade her questions. His eyes did not meet hers, instead they looked away from her down the Crescent, and a terrible fear gripped her. Suppose he suspected something—suppose he knew—something! Her very heart seemed to turn cold within her, to stay its beating as she watched his averted face. In a sudden accession of overwhelming terror she seized his arm.

"Mr. Cardyn, you do know something—you are keeping something from me. Tell me—tell me, anything—any certainty must be better than this awful suspense."

Cardyn did not answer for a moment. He did not turn his head or glance at her, he even drew his arm gently away.

"I do not know anything," he said slowly in a muffled tone that was curiously unlike anything Dorothy had heard from him before. "But I wonder—I expect I am quite wrong—I dare say I am going crazy—"

He moved slowly down the steps as he spoke, walking almost like a man in a dream. After a second's hesitation Dorothy followed him. She could not imagine what had caused the sudden change in his manner. There appeared to be nothing to account for it. The thought occurred to her that his mind had become unbalanced owing to the worry and the difficulties in connexion with Lady Anne's death.

The mode of his progression along the Crescent struck her as extraordinarily peculiar. He went forward a few steps, then stopped, then went forward again; once he turned his head and, seeing her behind him, seemed to hesitate for a moment, then went on more quickly, almost, thought Dorothy, as though he wanted to shake her off.

In spite of her all-absorbing anxiety the girl felt a curious little pang of pain. Then at last a strange thing happened. He hurried forward with a cry—Dorothy could not catch the words, but something about him, some cadence set her heart beating violently. She too sprang forward.

Bruce was stooping forward over the little beggar boy on the steps, then before Dorothy could catch him he had lifted the child tenderly in his arms and turned.

"Safe at last, Miss Dorothy," he said with a wry smile as the girl came up to him.

Dorothy could not believe the evidence of her own eyes and ears as she gazed at the limp figure lying in Cardyn's arms.

Could it indeed be Maureen—Maureen, her bright little butter-fly sister? Maureen in ragged coat and knickers, her pretty hair jagged round her forehead, her face dirty and tear-stained, her hands blackened and bleeding, her bare feet showing through her tattered shoes and stockings—but still, Maureen! With a half incredulous sound of joy Dorothy stretched out her arms.

Cardyn shook his head.

"She is too heavy for you. And—I think she is ill. I do not believe that she is quite conscious. I will carry her into the hall, and then—"

Dorothy uttered no further remonstrance. One glance at the fever-bright eyes that met hers unseeingly had filled her with an awful foreboding.

Cardyn went straight through the hall into the library and laid his burden down on the big sofa near the window; Dorothy knelt down and took the hot, dirty little hands in hers.

"Maureen—Maureen, darling, don't you know Dorothy?"

The blue fevered eyes focussed themselves on her face; a faint gleam of recognition dawned in them. The child tried to raise herself.

"Dor-othy," she said brokenly.

With a cry of joy Dorothy kissed the poor cracked lips.

But in another second Maureen had turned from her, had torn her hands from her sister's and apparently was fighting to keep off imaginary enemies with all her small strength.

Dorothy's eyes were full of a piteous appeal as she looked up at Cardyn. Then with a supreme effort she pulled herself together. She placed pillows under the child's head and laid her back gently on them and opened the window at her head.

"Please ring Dr. Spencer up and tell him to come at once," she said to Bruce. "And then to the hotel—to Margaret. They must get rooms ready. I know Dr. Spencer will say that Maureen must not stay here. It is this horrible, horrible house that is killing her!"

While Bruce was obeying her she got warm water and gently sponged the grime from the child's face and neck and arms, and took off her ragged garments, replacing them with a quilted dressing-gown of her own. For a time Maureen seemed more comfortable, but very soon she began to toss about again, to beat aimlessly on the air. She caught at Dorothy's skirt as she passed.

"Do you know who I am?" she asked in a harsh cracked voice absolutely unlike her own.

Dorothy touched the outstretched hand gently. "You are Maureen, my dear little sister," she said tenderly. "And I want you to lie still and go to sleep, just to please me."

But Maureen was past heeding her. She pushed her sister's hand away.

"I am not your little sister," she said in her high-pitched cracked child's voice. "I am not anybody's little sister. I am—shall I tell you what I am?—I am—only you must not tell anybody"—her voice dropping to a whisper so that they could scarcely hear—"because if you did they would perhaps hang me. I am"—in a hoarse strained tone—"the Cat Burglar!"

Dorothy gave a cry of horror.

"Maureen, darling, you must not."

Bruce Cardyn touched her. "Don't contradict her. She is wandering, poor child. She has heard so much of the murder and the Cat Burglar that it is haunting her brain."

At this moment the long-expected motor drove up to the door and the inspector and John Daventry got out. The Ferret was looking as imperturbable as ever. Daventry's face was as black as thunder.

"No use!" he said as Cardyn came into the hall. "Couldn't get a word out of the girl, do what we would."

"She is here," Cardyn said quietly.

"Who is here?" John Daventry questioned, staring at him.

"The child—Maureen."

John Daventry sat down heavily on the nearest chair. "How did she come?" he questioned helplessly. "Who found her?"

Cardyn smiled faintly. "I may say she found herself. She was sitting on a doorstep lower down the Crescent, disguised as a beggar boy."

"Good Lord!" ejaculated John Daventry, staring at him. "Of all the extraordinary things! Inspector, what is going to happen next in this case of yours?"

"The arrest of the criminal, hope," Inspector Furnival answered as he came forward, his face very stern and his eyes watching Cardyn's face carefully.

At the same moment Dr. Spencer walked into the hall.

"What is this I'm told? Little Miss Maureen found?"

Hearing his voice Dorothy came out of the library.

"Maureen is here, Dr. Spencer. But she is dreadfully ill. I don't think she even knows us, and she keeps on telling me that she is not Maureen —that she is the Cat Burglar! You must save her for me, doctor!"

"Tut, tut! my dear!" the doctor said, patting her arm paternally. "Children are up and down. I expect Maureen is overtired and probably overexcited by what she has gone through. We shall soon have her about again." He hurried after her into the library.

The three men left in the hall stood and looked at each other. Daventry was the first to speak.

"Let me catch the ruffians who stole little Maureen away, and by the Lord above I will strangle every mother's son of them. I will offer a big reward for every one who can give any information about them. How much shall it be, inspector? Five thousand?"

"Too much!" the inspector said laconically. "I think we shall clear the matter up for you in a day or two without a reward. The reward offered for the discovery of Lady Anne's murderer or murderers did not do much!"

"No! And you did not do much, either," retorted John Daventry. "I wouldn't mention that if were you, inspector."

"Ah, well, when we have found that mystery out and made *one* arrest I dare say you will be as much surprised as anyone, Mr. Daventry," said the inspector placidly.

"I shall be surprised if you arrest anyone, right or wrong, for my part!" John Daventry said. "Nice useful sort of lot you Scotland Yard men are!"

At this juncture Dr. Spencer came out of the library.

"I have phoned for an ambulance and nurses, Mr. Daventry—most convenient arrangement having the telephone in the library. The child must be taken to a nursing home without delay."

"What is the matter with her?" John Daventry asked bluntly.

The doctor regarded him over the top of his spectacles.

"Shock and exposure," he said briefly. "She will require great care for some time. I am having her moved to a nursing home close at hand. The sooner she is out of this house the better."

"Is she talking about the Cat Burglar?" John Daventry pursued.

"Yes! She is quite upsetting her sister," the doctor answered. "But my dear Mr. Daventry, it is worse than useless to talk about the wanderings of a sick child. Once away from here she will be better. No doubt she has heard people talking about the Cat Burglar, and her disordered imagination has fastened upon the idea. As for there being any relation in it to facts, the very notion is ridiculous. But there is one person I should like to see punished, inspector"—raising his voice for that gentleman's benefit—"and that is that housemaid, Alice."

"There I am with you, doctor," John Daventry joined in vigorously. "Girl deserves hanging."

CHAPTER XX

"Good morning, Mr. Soames! Lovely morning isn't it?"

The Daventry Arms, a picturesque black and white timbered inn, stood facing the village green. Opposite the inn door, between it and the pond where there would be water lilies later and where to-day the ducks were swimming lazily in the sunshine, there stood a very old yew tree with wooden seats round its gigantic trunk. Tradition had it that the second Charles had rested there when escaping from the soldiers of the Commonwealth. To-day a couple of old gaffers sat there smoking their pipes and exchanging remarks about the weather and the state of the crops with the landlord of the Daventry Arms.

That gentleman turned suddenly and his jaw dropped when he saw who his interlocutor was.

"This is a pleasure I had almost given up hoping for, Mr. Inspector, sir!"

"Oh, it hadn't left my mind that I promised to give you a call if I came this way," the inspector said easily. "And here I am, you see! And I'm sure it's a pleasure to see you in all your glory as the landlord of the Daventry Arms, Mr. Soames."

"Acting landlord, inspector," Soames corrected. "We haven't been getting on quite so quickly as you expected."

"You haven't indeed?" said the inspector. "But how is it, Mr. Soames? I thought that Mr. Daventry had promised—"

"Mr. John is doing everything he can for me, sir; he is backing me, and I don't think there is any doubt that the licence will be transferred to me at the next sessions. Only you see it isn't done yet. So I'm just having a preliminary canter, so to speak, until the licence of the Daventry Arms really stands in my name."

"I see." Inspector Furnival took out a large handkerchief and rubbed his forehead. "I see. It is astonishing how hot trudging along your country roads makes a man, and I have walked up from the station, for there was no sort of conveyance to be had. I hope you can give me a bite of lunch, Mr. Soames! I have heard great things of what the Daventry Arms can do in the culinary line."

"Have you really, sir? Well, how would a slice of cold beef with a salad suit you? And a bit of real Stilton to wind up? Or if you would care to wait there will be a couple of spring chickens and a slice of Yorkshire ham—"

"I think I will have the beef and Stilton," decided the inspector. "It will be ready quicker and there is no doubt that your country air gives one an appetite. And a glass of your best ale, Mr. Soames."

"Yes, sir. And you will find that it can't be beaten. If you will come with me—"

The inspector followed him into a big comfortable room overlooking an old-fashioned garden. It struck him that

Soames was looking decidedly older and thinner in spite of the fresh air. There was even less of the traditional portliness of the country landlord about him now than when he left Charlton Crescent. He himself brought in the ale for which the inspector had asked, and then began to lay the table in methodical fashion.

"And how do you like being back in your native place, Mr. Soames?" the inspector inquired. "It is your native place, isn't it?"

"Yes, sir! I was born in a cottage in the wood over yonder," pointing through the window to where beyond the garden there stretched an apparently endless vista of tree-tops. "My father was head gamekeeper to the late Squire Daventry and his father before him and my mother was maid to his mother— the Lady Elizabeth Brand she was before she married him."

"A good family record," commented the inspector. "Your family and the Daventry family have been connected for years and attached, I take it?"

Soames's eyelids flickered. "I should hardly presume to say that, sir. Though I hope we have been faithful servants."

"I am sure you have," the inspector said heartily. "You went straight into service at the Keep as soon as you left school, eh? Mr John Daventry was telling me"—improvising a little.

"Not quite, sir," Soames took up his tray and paused near the door. "When I first left school, I went for a time to a cousin of my mother's, a chemist up Islington way, but I couldn't stand the shop life and the stuffiness of London after the fresh air of Daventry. Then for a bit I was in the garden at the Keep. But I had no real bent that way, and when there was an opening for a boy up at the Keep, I took it and thought myself lucky. There I have been ever since, second footman, first footman, then butler. At the Keep I might have been now, but for her late ladyship deciding to live in London entirely when Mr. Christopher and Mr. Frank died, and Mr. John not having the means to keep up a proper establishment at the Keep, besides having their own servants."

It was a long speech for the ex-butler, and at its conclusion he glanced obliquely at the detective.

Inspector Furnival did not appear to be looking at him, however. He was admiring the old-fashioned flowers in the herbaceous border under the window.

"Very sweet they are!" he said, sniffing. "None of your new-fangled begonias and things will ever come up to what we remember in the old garden at home, Mr. Soames. Green roses are the last thing they tell me, but give me an old-fashioned moss rose or a cabbage before all the green roses that ever were blown!"

"I agree with you, sir," Soames said as he opened the door. "Old-fashioned flowers and old-fashioned ways are the best in my opinion."

"There I am with you; and so was Lady Anne, wasn't she?" the inspector questioned, turning sharply.

Soames put his tray on a table near the door. "Yes. My lady always liked things best as they were in Queen Victoria's days. I must see after the cheese myself, sir. The Stilton I don't allow anyone else to touch."

"No hurry!" said the inspector genially. "I want a bit of a chat with you first, Mr. Soames. It will give a fillip to my appetite."

Though the words were spoken smoothly enough and though they were accompanied by a smile that showed the inspector's somewhat yellow teeth, there was an underlying note of authority.

Soames's ears were sharp enough to recognize it. He paused with his hand on the door-handle.

"Yes, sir. Of course I always enjoy a chat myself," he said with an obvious difficulty in keeping his voice steady.

"I saw your friend, Miss Pirnie, the other day," the inspector began.

The relief in Soames's expression was obvious.

"Did you, sir? I hope she was looking well? I have not heard of her for some little time. In fact I was thinking of running up to town as soon as I could spare a day, to see how things were going with her."

"She is looking first-rate," said the inspector. "I was talking to her about Lady Anne's pearls. I don't know whether you are aware that there is a rumour, growing stronger every day, that Lady Anne herself sold her pearls to Spagnum's? Miss Pirnie was very indignant about it."

"And I don't wonder," said Soames, his face turning red with anger. "My lady would never have done a thing of that kind. She was far too proud. If she had wanted to sell her pearls she would have done so. But she would never have pretended they had been stolen! If you had known her ladyship—"

"Mr. Soames," said the detective sharply, "who did take the pearls?"

Soames met his eyes steadily enough. "I don't know, sir. I have never been able to guess. It has been the thing that has puzzled me the most of everything in the whole affair—who could have taken my lady's pearls."

For a moment Inspector Furnival did not speak. His small grey eyes focused themselves on Soames, held the unfortunate ex-butler's gaze as a snake's does a bird's. At last he said very deliberately with a pause between each word:

"Does it puzzle you, for instance, more than this question: Who killed Lady Anne Daventry?"

The unhappy Soames lost his usually florid colouring as if by a stroke, his face turned a dull, ashy white; the cheeks a little while ago so plump and rosy looked now in the clear midday light pendulous and yellow.

"I—er—oh—sir—" he stammered thickly.

The inspector's eyes still kept their cruel watch, probing, searching as though they would wring the truth out of the soul of the unhappy man before him. No answer came to his question, only that gibbering, moaning, stammering. Then as suddenly as it had begun the inspector's scrutiny stopped. He looked away from the almost convulsed face of the man before him, and drank in a long draught of the pure air coming in from the outside.

Released, Soames dropped heavily into the nearest chair; after staring at the inspector for a moment, he began to breathe in hoarse, painful gasps, wiping the sweat from his brow as he did so.

"I—don't—know—what you mean," he said at last, recovering himself somewhat.

The inspector looked back at him with a benevolent smile.

"Mean?" he echoed. "Mean, my dear Mr. Soames? I think it is I who should put that question to you. I mean just what I said. It did occur to me as curious that with all the mystery surrounding the death of Lady Anne Daventry you should say that the thing that puzzled you the most was the theft of Lady Anne's pearls! Now of the minor puzzles of the affair I find the disappearance of the pearls the least baffling."

Soames was sitting now facing the inspector and still breathing grampus-fashion, one hand firmly planted on each knee. Very gradually the colour was coming back to his face; it was far from reaching its usual rubicund proportions, but the ghastly pallor that had been called up by the inspector's question had passed. He looked up now in obviously genuine surprise.

"Do you mean that you know who it was took them, sir?"

"Ah! That would be telling," the inspector said with the same open smile. "You will soon know how, Mr. Soames. Things are moving rapidly to a climax, and all the world will be told the secret of the house in Charlton Crescent before long. But what I want to know now is—"

He paused dramatically.

The colour that was stealing back to Soames's face began to ebb slowly away again. He sat gazing at the inspector in an odd, frightened fashion.

"Yes, yes? What you want to know is—?" he prompted.

The inspector took out a cigar case. "Smoking is not forbidden here? No? Then you will try one of these, Mr. Soames. They were given me by a grateful client. Very good they are. You won't? Oh, well perhaps, you are wise—before lunch. Yes. What I should like to know above all things at this present moment is, who made the footmarks on the border under the window? The window you found open, you will remember, Mr. Soames?"

There was no doubt that Soames did remember. This time his face did not turn white. He became instead a curious mottled purple.

"I suppose the murderer must have been concealed in the house and managed to get out that way. I have always thought—"

"Ah! I see you have decided that the murderer was not one of the five, as some people call them?" the inspector said in a chaffing tone that seemed to affect Soames more than his previous sternness.

The butler glared round wildly as if seeking some way of escape.

"It—it doesn't seem possible that it could be, sir."

"It doesn't, does it?" the inspector went on chattily. "Yet the murderer must have been some one in the house—"

"Concealed in the house," Soames muttered.

"I scarcely think so," said the inspector, taking a seat on the table near the unhappy man. "At least if he made the footmarks in the border he must have been in the house afterwards, because—"

He made another of his telling pauses. Soames wriggled uneasily in a fashion irresistibly suggestive of the toad under the harrow.

"Because—or perhaps I had better say," the inspector corrected, "that at any rate if he got out of the house himself he left his boots behind him. They have been found upstairs among some of the things left by Lady Anne's son Frank."

Soames stared at him helplessly. Twice he opened his mouth as if to speak and closed it again fishwise. At last he said thickly:

"Well, Mr. Frank—he could not have worn the boots, and Mr. John and me—we couldn't have got them on to save our lives. I don't believe there was a man in the house that could."

"I dare say not," the inspector acquiesced blandly, his small ferret eyes fixed upon the ex-butler's twitching face. "But then you see, Mr. Soames, I do not imagine they were worn by a man. But I *do* think that the time has come for you to speak out and tell the truth."

CHAPTER XXI

"CHARLTON CRESCENT MYSTERY! Astounding Story!"

Walking quickly down a side street near Charlton Crescent, Inspector Furnival was greeted by the foregoing placard.

"*Daily Mercury,* Midday Edition—that's the racing edition," he said to himself. "Umph! They must think they have got hold of something good, if they find room for anything but lists of probable winners and wires from the course!"

He took a paper from the boy and unfolded it as he walked.

"Charlton Crescent Mystery—Astounding development!" figured largely on the front page.

"Now, what the deuce have they got hold of?" he said to himself as he turned to it. "Oh, by Jove!" His face clouded over as he read.

At the moment of going to press an extraordinary story has been brought to our notice. A witness from Queensland, whose good faith we have no reason to doubt, has identified Bruce Cardyn, the secretary, as Bruce Daventry Balmaine, only son of Robert and Marjorie Balmaine—Mrs. Balmaine being, of course, the Miss Marjorie Daventry who has often been mentioned in the course of the Charlton Crescent case. She was the daughter of the late Squire Daventry by his first wife and thus step-daughter of the murdered Lady Anne. She or her children, should she leave any, inherit largely at Lady Anne's death under the old Squire's will. Until now it has been supposed that she left only one daughter, the Miss Margaret Balmaine so often mentioned in the history of the case, but it has now been proved beyond doubt that her son also survived her, and is now known as Bruce Cardyn, the secretary. His assumption of the name of Cardyn is explained by the fact that his father adopted the name of Cardyn by deed of poll on coming in to some money on the death of a distant relative. But why Mr. Bruce Cardyn entered Lady Anne Daventry's service as secretary, and why he and his sister, Miss Margaret Balmaine, appear to have decided to conceal their relationship seems to us to call for explanation. The matter has been placed in the hands of the police and further developments may be expected shortly.

The inspector drew a long breath when he had finished.

"So that's that! The fat is in the fire with a vengeance! Well, it will quicken matters up a bit, that's one good job!"

He squared his shoulders as he walked along quickly. For once his usual immobile face showed signs of inward perturbation. He turned into the first post-office he came to and despatched several messages, then he went quickly on to the house in Charlton Crescent. As he went up the steps the rector of North Coton opened the door.

"You there, inspector! I was just looking for you. What does this mean?" He was holding a copy of the paper the inspector had been reading. As he spoke he tapped the offending paragraph. The inspector drew him back into the house.

"I suppose you had no idea of this, Mr. Fyvert?"

"Not the least. How could I have?" the reverend gentleman said testily. "Do you mean that you—?"

"I discovered it very early in the case," the inspector assented, leading the way to the library. "Naturally I inquired into the antecedents of every one in the room, and the fact that Mr. Bruce Cardyn was old Squire Daventry's grandson was not particularly difficult to find out."

Mr. Fyvert laid his hat on the library table, and stood gazing at the inspector in consternation.

"But you do not see the difference this makes? Personally, I have hitherto regarded Bruce Cardyn as one who might really be put out of the question. Now—"

"Now?" the inspector prompted.

Mr. Fyvert spread out his hands.

"My dear sir, is it not obvious? Bruce Cardyn, inheriting as he does under the will of my brother-in-law, largely, at the death, had as strong, possibly a stronger motive for the—er—murder than any one else."

"I see that, of course. It jumps to the eyes," the inspector agreed quietly.

"Then, once you know that, his whole conduct seems suspicious," the rector of North Coton went on hotly. "Why did he go to my sister as secretary-detective, or whatever it was, without telling her he was poor Daventry's grandson? A false name, too—it will take a lot of explaining as far as I am concerned, let me tell you."

"Oh, well, the name was his own, as you see in the paper," the inspector said quietly. "It was not Cardyn's fault that Lady Anne did not know of the change his father had made. Then, again, it was not his doing that Lady Anne applied to the firm of inquiry agents of which he was a member. That he attended her personally was, of course, his choice. He explained it to me by saying that when he saw Lady Anne had no idea of his identity he thought he would take the opportunity of seeing his mother's old home and possibly of making friends with the family. He knew with what distaste his father and mother's marriage had always been regarded by the Daventrys and he had no idea that he inherited anything under the Squire's will. Got the idea out of a story-book, I should think, I told him. But there you are!"

"There I am not!" said the rector emphatically. "I call it a foolish attempt to explain what is unexplainable. And why did he and his sister pretend not to recognize one another? There is something behind all this that you have not found out yet, inspector. It looks to me like a deep-laid plot between the two. Though I can't believe that Margaret—However, I am going straight back to the hotel to tax her with all this duplicity and to hear what she has to say."

"I must ask you not to do that," the inspector said, taking a few paces up and down the room, his hands clasped behind him, his head bent, his brows drawn together. At last he came to a standstill before the rector again. "Give me twenty-four hours, sir, and I think I shall be able to explain all that now seems mysterious to you. Will you give me your word not to speak to Miss Balmaine on the subject until this time has expired?"

"What is the good of it if I do?" the rector questioned impatiently. "Won't the girl see it stuck up on every poster, buy a paper and know that the game, whatever it is, is up?"

"It won't be stuck up on every poster. I have taken care of that," the inspector returned placidly. "At present this story is a scoop of the *Daily Mercury*'s, and will remain so until there is no more need for secrecy."

"Well, well! I don't see the sense of it, but as you are in charge of the case I suppose I am bound to respect your wishes," conceded the rector unwillingly. "Only for twenty-four hours, though, mind! Then I shall take the liberty of speaking to Miss Margaret, and giving her a piece of my mind."

"As you like, sir. When I have had time for what I want to do."

But the inspector's long-drawn breath of relief did not escape the rector of North Coton. He frowned severely as he turned and walked out of the house without another word.

Left alone, the inspector waited by the table a minute, drawing his brows together apparently in a brown study, then he turned to a box that stood at the end of the table, and began to look over the contents, a heterogeneous mass of grey muslin, white paper and bits of grey parchment. Finally he selected a square piece of the parchment signed at both ends and a piece of charred paper on which a few words were still visible. He scrutinized these for a few minutes through a small microscope, then carefully wrapped them up in tissue paper, and put them in his pocket. He locked the box and as he went out of the room carefully locked the door. In the hall he spoke a few words to the man on duty. Outside the house he paused a moment and looked at his watch.

"No time to spare!" he said to himself as he hailed a passing taxi and bade the man drive to 161 Ilford Road, Fulham. They took the nearest way, through the park. And though Inspector Furnival's keen eyes took note of everything he passed his mind was busy with the puzzles of that bewildering mystery of the house in Charlton Crescent.

Ilford Road was one of the maze of small streets that lie at the back of Fulham Road. No 161 was one of a long row of depressing looking houses, all built after the same pattern. No. 161 differed a little from its neighbours in that its knocker and the fanlight over the door were a little cleaner.

As the inspector rang the bell, two men in plain clothes appeared as if by magic from the corner of a side street close at hand and at the same moment a policeman strolled by. He touched his hat to the inspector just as the door was opened by a tousled-looking elderly woman.

"Mr. Branksome at home?" asked the inspector.

"No! He is never at home in the daytime."

"Mrs. Branksome here?" the inspector went on sharply.

"No. I know nothing about her," the woman returned truculently.

The inspector glanced at her. "Show me his rooms," he said briefly.

The woman stared at him, tried to close the door—an effort the inspector frustrated by putting out his foot.

"Mr. Branksome ain't fond of having folks in his rooms when he's at home. It's no good you trying to get there when he is out," she said defiantly, pushing the door hard upon the inspector's foot the while.

"I am from Scotland Yard, my good woman," the inspector said, handing her his card and at the same time beckoning to the policeman who was apparently watching the proceedings with interest. He gave the man a few low-toned directions.

"Now, madam," he said, turning back, "the rooms at once, please."

The woman made no further objection. She let the door open and slipped back against the wall with a half-sob.

"I can't stop you, but I have always been a respectable woman myself. I never had the police coming to my house."

The inspector stopped and looked at her.

"I think, madam, I had the pleasure of making your acquaintance in Kensington a few years ago. There was a little charge of shop-lifting. Mrs. Glover your name was then, if I remember rightly. No need to mention more, I see. The rooms, please."

The landlady's face had turned as white as chalk.

"The drawing-room suite, first floor," she said, her breath coming unevenly.

The inspector waited for no more. He went up two stairs at a time. The drawing-room suite evidently consisted of a small, dingily furnished, drab-looking little sitting-room and a small scantily furnished bedroom behind. At first sight there was nothing to differentiate it from hundreds of lodgings in the same sort of house in London, but the inspector's keen eyes saw that a wooden cupboard in the corner of the sitting-room and a box in the corner of the bedroom had both been fitted with extra strong locks. Not strong, enough, however, to resist a certain little instrument the inspector took from his pocket. Very soon the contents of the box were at his mercy and the inspector gave a satisfied grunt as his flexible fingers ran through them and separated them. Some curious articles were at the top—a mass of white hair; what looked like a woman's bonnet; underneath, a long old-fashioned cloak of black silk. Then again under that many papers and letters. The inspector glanced through them casually and selected one or two.

Then he drew out a large photograph in a handsome tooled leather frame—a photograph of a pretty, smiling, fair girl, in a remarkably *décolleté* gown. "Yours always, Daisy," was scrawled across it.

The inspector grinned. "I wonder what Miss Daisy will say when she sees this," he said to himself.

CHAPTER XXII

IT WAS CURIOUS how often Bruce Cardyn's steps took him past the nursing home in FitzGeorge Square where Maureen Fyvert was being slowly nursed back to health. In whatever part of London his business lay, the way home was always by

FitzGeorge Square. It was but very seldom, however, that he was rewarded by the sight of the sick child's sister or any sign of her. To-night, he had been busy all day on some work for his partner, for of late Inspector Furnival's demand on his time had been less insistent. The poster and the *Daily Mercury* had naturally not escaped his notice, and it seemed to him that the detective's insistent advice had turned out as badly as it well could, and he had his own reasons for disliking the discovery of his identity to occur at this present juncture.

The inspector was still busy most days. That the mystery surrounding Lady Anne Daventry's death was rapidly being cleared up, Bruce knew. The bits of the puzzle, as the inspector termed it, were fitting into one another. But the major mystery remained a mystery to Cardyn yet. That certain suspicions had presented themselves went without saying. One possibility there was that would keep recurring to his mind, only to be dismissed with shuddering horror.

As he took the turning leading into the Square he saw a familiar figure approaching.

Dorothy was walking very quickly and her face bore manifest traces of disturbance. She had got quite near him before he was recognized. Then he saw her hesitate a moment as if she were going to turn back. He quickened his steps.

"Miss Fyvert, I was hoping to see you!"

"Oh!" The girl distinctly drew away from him now and regarded him with cool unfriendly eyes. "And why should you wish to see me—Mr.—er—Cardyn—er—Balmaine? Really, I do not know what to call you now." Then in a moment she saw the obvious opening she had given him and turned away biting her lip.

But it was too late to retrieve her error.

"My name is Bruce Balmaine Cardyn as it always was," the man said quietly. "And I should be very grateful if you would call me Bruce. After all, we are a sort of cousins, are we not?"

Dorothy shook her head.

"No! No, Mr. Balmaine Cardyn—no! Really there is not even a connexion between us. I couldn't really believe that a cousin of mine could turn detective."

"Well, I do not want to be your cousin," he said daringly. "I should prefer another relationship, Dorothy."

The girl put out her hand. "Please don't— now—"

"Later!" Bruce assented daringly.

Dorothy's eyes were full of unshed tears.

"I can't think of anything but Maureen now. At least I shouldn't, only—what does this mean!" She held out an opened letter to him.

Cardyn glanced at it. It was not dated, he noticed at once; probably, he thought quickly, that Dorothy should have no opportunity of refusing the interview.

DEAR MADAM,

I shall do myself the honour of calling upon you at your hotel this evening about seven o'clock if you will be good enough to give me a few minutes conversation.

Yours obediently,

J.F. FURNIVAL.

"Oh, do try and keep him away!" Dorothy urged, tears springing into her brown eyes. "I, —it makes me ill to see him— that horrid man! I know that it was his prying about the house that made Maureen—"

"How is she?" Cardyn questioned as she waited, looking up at him imploringly.

"I think she is better," Dorothy said slowly. "She knows us all, and she is not delirious and only talks about the Cat Burglar in her sleep. But she is so frightfully weak. She can hardly lift her hand to her head, and she lies so quietly and so still, only looking at you with such big frightened eyes, that I can hardly believe that the pale child on the pillows is Maureen."

"Poor child!" Cardyn said sympathetically. "Has she said anything about Alice Gray or told you where she was those two days?"

"She has told us nothing—nothing at all!" Dorothy answered with a little quiver in her voice. "And the doctor says that we are not to ask her anything or talk of anything exciting before her. In her sleep, as I said, she talks of the Cat Burglar. And sometimes she cries so piteously and begs us not to let her go to prison—either of us, she always says. I suppose she means herself and Alice. Mr. Cardyn, do you think her mind dwells on those fearful stories of that wretched Cat Burglar, simply because she has heard them talked about? You do not—do not think she could have had anything to do with—with helping him to murder Lady Anne?"

Of course not!" Cardyn beckoned to a passing taxi. "Miss Fyvert, you will let me see you to the hotel. I may be able to help you with the inspector." For a wonder Dorothy made no objection, but stepped meekly into the taxi. Cardyn seated himself opposite.

"Miss Fyvert, you must not worry about the nonsense your little sister talks. That she got into bad hands when she struck up a friendship with Alice Gray is indisputable, but that either of the two had any part in Lady Anne Daventry's murder is impossible, unbelievable."

Dorothy felt vaguely comforted. Once more Bruce Cardyn seemed to have turned from the detective she despised into the kind stranger who had rescued her from the fire, and of whom she had so often secretly dreamt during the past two years.

"But if it is not about Maureen, what do you think he wants to see me for?" she questioned after a time.

Bruce was quick to notice the difference in her tone. He had never heard that note in it since the inspector had disclosed his real occupation to her.

"I do not know," he said slowly after a pause, during which he had silently gazed at the houses they were so swiftly passing. "Inspector Furnival has not given me his confidence in any way, but I should think—I should imagine that it might be about that letter that was found in the escritoire—the one from you to Lady Anne, I mean."

"In which I asked her for money?" Dorothy questioned, her tones hardening. "I suppose he wants to know why I wanted it and how I got it."

"I should think it more than probable," Bruce assented.

"I shall not tell him," Dorothy said defiantly. "Why should I?"

"Well, it is not wise to make an enemy of the inspector, you know," said Bruce diplomatically.

"It cannot possibly matter to him why I wanted the money. I didn't get it," the girl argued.

"No. That is perhaps why he wants to question you," Bruce said quietly. "Miss Fyvert, don't you see that in a case like this the police are bound to inquire into everything—even the veriest trifle that may have any bearing upon it? You will only at the most delay matters by opposing the inspector. It will all come out in the end. I know—I am certain that you have nothing to be ashamed of. Why not trust the inspector?"

"Because I hate him—loathe him!" Dorothy exclaimed with sudden warmth. "Detestable man! He dared to hint to me that my need of money might have been supplied by stealing Lady Anne's pearls and selling them! I believe he is capable of saying that I murdered her too. Now if it had been you—" She stopped short with a quick look that set all Bruce's pulses thrilling.

"If I asked you, would you trust me?" he questioned gravely.

Dorothy hesitated a minute, then she stretched out her hand.

"I have been a beast all the time—an ungrateful beast," she said impulsively. "But I will trust you—I do trust you. I will tell you all about it—you will not fail me."

Bruce held the slender ungloved hand for a moment in his firm, strong clasp.

"If you will honour me with your confidence I promise to respect it in every way and in any circumstance," he said quietly.

"Well, then I will," Dorothy said with the air of one coming to a sudden decision. "It—it really isn't my own secret. That was one reason why I did not tell it at once. I had lost money at cards, certainly, but my half-sister, Mrs. St. John Lavis, had lost much more. Her husband is poor, and naturally was very angry when she ran him into debt. He had forbidden her to play cards the last time he paid up for her losses, and threatened to advertise that he was not responsible if she did it again. He would have done it too. He is just the sort of man who would. And then Mona would have been ruined. Nobody would have trusted her in the shops or anywhere. And of course, that would have done for her socially even in the present day. I don't really think that morals matter so much as money nowadays," she finished, looking at him with wet eyes.

"Some people put money before everything," Bruce acquiesced. "Then it was really on Mrs. Lavis's behalf that you appealed to Lady Anne?"

"Yes, of course! There was nobody else I could ask. And I thought—I did think Aunt Anne cared for me enough to help me. But you see she wouldn't. Then, I don't know what we should have done, but my mother had left us some jewels we were to sell only in case of great extremity. My share was an emerald necklace with a diamond enamel pendant. A cousin of ours had always admired it and was willing to give a fancy price for it. So we sold it to her and paid Mona's debts."

"Why did not Mrs. Lavis sell her share instead of yours?" Bruce questioned.

"Ah, well, my cousin would only have bought the emeralds, you see. Besides—" Dorothy's voice sank—"Mona had disposed of hers before I appealed to Lady Anne. That was only a last resource. I didn't really think the emeralds would have fetched as much as they did."

"Then there was the fifty-pound note that you gave to your dressmaker, and that was one of those paid by Messrs. Spagnum for the pearls?" Bruce suggested.

"I have never been able to understand that," Dorothy said, meeting his gaze openly. "Aunt Anne gave it to me as my half-year's allowance."

"You are quite sure it was the same note?" Bruce asked after thinking a minute.

"Oh, I think so," Dorothy said, considering the question. "I didn't take the number, but it looked just the same. I put it in my writing-case and locked it up, so of course it must have been."

"If your writing-case had just one of those ordinary little locks it might quite easily have been changed. How long did you leave it in the case?"

"Oh, not long. Only until the next day, believe. I wasn't particularly well-off just then. And I owed Madame Benoit a good deal of it so I took it to her at once. So there wasn't much time to change it, you see. Besides, who would want to do it?"

"Ah? That is the question!" Bruce responded, his eyes looking away from the fair face of the girl opposite, mechanically watching the passing traffic. "The obvious answer is the person who stole the pearls, of course."

"Oh! But that must have been a burglar, some one outside the house," Dorothy objected.

Cardyn did not answer for a minute, then he said very deliberately:

"Some one in the house took Lady Anne's diary from the escritoire. Some one in the house took and could have explained the mystery of the pearls."

"I don't see that," Dorothy said obstinately. "If—if the Cat Burglar got up to the window and murdered Lady Anne, I don't know why he shouldn't have opened my writing-case and changed the note."

"Where did he get the other one from?" Cardyn questioned. "The one that Messrs. Spagnum gave the thief?"

"Well, naturally, I suppose he stole the pearls and got the note himself and put it into my case."

"That implies that the thief knew you had a fifty-pound note there," Cardyn argued. "And it makes it practically certain that it was some one in the house. The Cat Burglar could not have known."

"I am not so sure," Dorothy said doubtfully. "He seems such an omnipresent sort of person, don't you think?"

"He would be, if he did everything that was put down to him," Bruce observed dryly. "Now, Miss Fyvert, you will trust me to respect your confidence. But at the same time you will allow me to explain matters to the inspector if absolutely necessary?"

"Yes—I suppose so," Dorothy hesitated. "I had ever so much rather you did not tell him, though. It is so different with you. You see, knowing you beforehand—I—er—looking upon you as a friend—"

They were nearing the hotel where the Fyverts were staying now. As the driver began to slow down, threading his way through the traffic, Bruce leaned forward.

"It is my dearest hope that you will continue to trust me—to look upon me as a friend," he said earnestly. "The time is close at hand now when everything will be cleared up. And then—then may I perhaps dare to ask for more than friendship—Dorothy. I wonder whether you will give it to me?"

But the girl's eyes did not meet his. She drew away into the corner of the taxi.

"I don't know," she said lamely. "I can't even think of things now. I can't decide anything."

She sprang out of the taxi, pushing aside Cardyn's proffered hand, and hurried into the hotel. Cardyn followed more slowly. She did not pause in the lounge, but almost ran upstairs.

Bruce stood looking after her for a minute, then as he turned he met the quizzical gaze of Inspector Furnival.

"The young lady seems to be in a hurry. I am glad to see you, though, Mr. Cardyn. You will be quite valuable as an assistant at the interview I have arranged." He glanced at his watch. "Yes, I thought the time was getting on. Come along, Mr. Cardyn, the scene is set for the first scene in the final drama."

He turned to the staircase, Bruce accompanying him, then stopped and beckoned to a man standing near the door, a man whom Bruce recognized as one of the inspector's satellites. He was carrying an oddly shaped parcel, wrapped carelessly in brown paper.

The thought struck Cardyn that it looked like an old countrywoman's luggage. Rack his brains as he would he could not make out what it contained.

The three of them proceeded up the stairs and a little way along the corridor at the top. There the inspector opened the door of a small sitting-room—evidently private, and, motioning

Bruce to enter, took the parcel from his man, at the same time saying a few words in an undertone. Bruce caught the last sentence—"As soon as it comes, mind. Let there be no mistake."

CHAPTER XXIII

DOROTHY FYVERT walked quickly into the room. Cardyn got the impression that she had waited outside lacking the courage to enter, and then, rallying her self-control by a supreme effort, had come in with a rush. He made a step forward, but she did not glance at him. Her brown eyes sought the inspector's and, meeting his, stayed there with a terrified expression.

"You wanted to speak to me?" she said nervously.

The inspector did not answer for a minute. Apparently he was listening to some distant sound. At last he spoke.

"Yes. I wished to speak to you and to Miss Balmaine. A certain piece of new evidence has been obtained which might bear distinctly on the matter of Lady Anne Daventry's death, and I should like to know what you both have to say about it."

"What is it?" Dorothy questioned curtly.

"You shall know in a minute," the inspector promised. "Miss Balmaine will be here directly. We will wait for her."

As he spoke his eyes strayed to the brown paper parcel which he had deposited under a small table and of which only one corner was to be seen.

He had scarcely finished speaking when Margaret Balmaine opened the door. She looked a curious contrast to Dorothy, whose pallor and general look of anxiety had been accentuated by the inspector's note. Miss Balmaine had returned to the make-up which she had temporarily discarded at the time of Lady Anne's death. She was wearing to-day a frock of pale grey marocain, exquisitely embroidered in silver beads, and caught up at one side with an old silver and crystal clasp. The gown was very short as to sleeves and skirt, very low as to neck, but the throat and arms so generously revealed were beautifully modelled, the legs and feet in their nude silk stockings and grey suede shoes were without flaw. But Cardyn could not help feeling as he had often felt before that it was a thousand pities that Margaret Balmaine with undeniable good looks should resort to such very obvious artificial means to enhance them. The pink and white of her cheeks, the darkness of her eyebrows and eyes, even the sheen of her shingled golden hair were all, quite evidently, due to art. Yet in spite of everything, in spite of the ready smile with which she greeted the inspector, Cardyn could not help fancying that he saw some intangible traces of disturbance on her face.

"Well inspector," she began, in her old half defiant manner. "What is this very serious business that you want to see me upon? Have you found out who killed Lady Anne, or who abducted Maureen?"

"Both, I hope, Miss—er—Balmaine," the inspector answered her quietly, the gravity of his tone contrasting curiously with the lightness of hers.

Meeting his eyes, it seemed to Cardyn that the girl visibly winced.

"I am very glad to hear it!" she said in the same tone. "You have been long enough about it, have you not? And who is guilty, inspector?" This time the anxiety in her tone was obvious.

The inspector did not choose to satisfy it.

"All in good time! All in good time! I have just a few questions to ask you young ladies now before we say any more."

"Oh, but, inspector," Dorothy interposed, "if you have found out about Maureen—I—really must know—"

"Oh, well, the Brighton police traced that without much difficulty," the inspector answered. "It seems that Alice Gray got into conversation with some young man on the esplanade. There were some travelling musicians on the beach and a gipsy fortune-teller with a van behind, and little Miss Maureen began to dance to the music with the other children. Of course, trained as she had been she attracted the notice of the fortune-teller, who appears to have thought there was money to be made out of abducting her. She persuaded her to get into the van and drove off. Then, learning from the papers later who the child was, I suppose she thought more money would be obtained by waiting—or she fancied she would be safer if the girl were dressed up as a boy. She came up to London to some horrible haunt in the East End, and I suppose the child escaped from there and managed to find her way back to Charlton Crescent. The shock of it all acting upon her when she was already in bad health seems to have been too much for her brain. That is what I make of it. But of positive ill treatment there was none."

"Thank you." Dorothy turned away to the window. The inspector's words had relieved her of a horrible dread.

Margaret Balmaine waited. Her head was thrown back. Cardyn saw that one of her hands, hanging down by her side, was clenching and unclenching itself nervously.

The inspector, too, waited for a minute. His face was very stern as he glanced from one girl to the other. At last he seemed to be satisfied.

He drew from its hiding-place the brown paper parcel that he had brought into the room, and set it on the table. Dorothy turned towards him, moving slowly as if drawn against her will, staring at the parcel. Margaret Balmaine's eyes followed his every movement as if fascinated. The inspector took a knife from his pocket and, opening it, set about cutting the string and unwrapping the paper with exasperating slowness.

Cardyn scarcely knew what he expected, but certainly he was not prepared to see the inspector lift out with meticulous care just a milliner's cardboard box and then from that an old-fashioned black silk bonnet. Inspector Furnival held this up in his hand for a minute, apparently surveying it with the greatest interest, while from beneath his lowered eyelids his keen little eyes went from one to the other of the motionless faces of the girls before him.

"Very like a bonnet of Lady Anne Daventry's," he shot out a last. "But—not Lady Anne's!"

Dead silence followed. Neither girl moved. At last Dorothy drew a long breath. Margaret Balmaine might have been carved out of stone, so absolutely motionless was she. The inspector's eyes relaxed their scrutiny. He made another dive into the box and produced a white wig, evidently dressed in imitation of

Lady Anne's own beautiful snow-white hair. At sight of it Dorothy shuddered violently and clutched at the table, shivering from head to foot.

"Oh, what does it mean? What does it mean?" she cried.

Not one muscle of Margaret Balmaine's face stirred. Even the hand by her side was still now. Cardyn's eyes watching closely saw that the knuckles were showing white through the tightening skin. Then he looked away from her to the girl he loved. There could be no doubt that Dorothy was frightened—horribly frightened. Her pretty brown eyes were wide open, dilated and staring at the mass of hair in the inspector's hand with a horrible fixity. Her mouth was twitching, too; more than once she moistened her dry lips with her tongue. Cardyn made a step towards her, as if to range himself on her side to protect her. But she put out her hand and motioned him back imperatively.

"What does it mean?" she questioned hoarsely. "I—I can't understand."

There was another pause. Then the inspector said in the quick curt tones that cut across the tragic atmosphere of the room like a knife:

"It means that we have always suspected, that undoubtedly some one has, on one occasion, if not more, successfully impersonated Lady Anne Daventry. I asked for this interview in order to see whether either of you two ladies could help me to discover the guilty person."

"Of course we can't—we told you we knew nothing about the theft of the pearls," Dorothy said, that painful twitching of her mouth extending to her throat, the straining of her muscles plainly visible.

Margaret Balmaine stepped quietly to her side.

"Do not frighten yourself, Dorothy. Don't you see that the inspector—*knows*? May I ask Inspector Furnival how long it has been allowed to introduce the customs of France into our judicial procedure? Though I believe that in the neighbouring country the examination takes place before a magistrate, so that there is at least some semblance of fairness. But here you try to frighten two defenceless girls into incriminating themselves. Take away your pieces of accusation, inspector"—pointing to the wig and the bonnet—"you will not find out anything here."

The words were a defiance, her manner, her gesture were superb. In spite of all that Cardyn knew, in spite of that further at which he only guessed, he felt a quick throb of admiration as he looked at her, at the small, uplifted star-like head.

It was evident that her colour beneath her makeup had not varied. Her eyes were clear and steady and full of scorn as she looked at the inspector.

"Well, what are you going to do? It does not seem to have struck you that there have been other well-dressed old ladies in the world besides Lady Anne Daventry, and possibly those things"—pointing at them contemptuously—"have been worn to impersonate someone quite different. Or they may just be 'properties' worn by some actress."

"I fancy they were," the inspector interposed quietly.

He moved nearer the two girls as he spoke. Dorothy backed against the wall. The horror in her eyes had deepened during the inspector's brief colloquy with Margaret. She gazed helplessly from one to the other.

"Where did you find those things?" Margaret questioned him.

"Ah I thought that might interest you," the inspector answered as he put his hand into the box again and drew out this time a strange, staring-looking object—a rough mask, such as are worn on Guy Fawkes day. From it there dangled long wisps of dirty white muslin.

"Another property," he observed dryly. "You do not seem interested, Miss Balmaine. And yet you would like to know where the wig and the bonnet were found. Well, I have been searching in strange places. The first two properties"—repeating the last word with sarcastic emphasis—"were found—" He stopped, and this time his gaze was fixed wholly upon Margaret Balmaine.

The tenseness of her attitude did not alter, but Cardyn caught a momentary flicker of her eyelids.

"Where were they found?" she questioned.

"In an apartment house in Ilford Road, Fulham," the inspector finished. "In a room occupied for the time being by Lady Anne's late secretary, Mr. David Branksome."

There was no mistaking the effect his words produced. A sort of quiver of relief passed over Dorothy's face. Some of the tension and the strain died out, a faint tinge of colour came back to the pale cheeks.

Margaret Balmaine started, for one second she set her small white teeth hard in her lip. Then she passed her handkerchief over it quickly.

"I don't believe it!" she flashed out.

The inspector shrugged his shoulders.

"I am afraid that belief or unbelief cannot affect hard facts."

Miss Balmaine flashed an angry glance at him. She had begun a defiant rejoinder when there was an interruption. There was a loud, insistent knock at the door.

Cardyn was about to open it, but the inspector was before him. A waiter with a familiar-looking yellow envelope on his salver stood in the passage.

"Telegram, sir, just come!"

The inspector took it and with a word of thanks shut the door. Then he tore the envelope open, while the other three stared at him breathlessly. An expression of relief was on his face as he glanced up.

"This is from North Hackney," he said quietly. "David Branksome was arrested there at four o'clock this afternoon."

CHAPTER XXIV

"ARRESTED! It is not true!" Margaret Balmaine's voice rang across the stillness that followed the inspector's words like a trumpet.

"Quite true!" said the inspector blandly. "Why do you say it is not?"

"Because he is not guilty. I know he is not," the girl said hotly.

"And how can you know that?" the inspector went on.

"Because he was miles away! I know he was!" Miss Balmaine reiterated.

"Miles away from—where—when?" the inspector questioned incisively.

Looking at him, his subordinates would have said that he was getting dangerous now.

"From that house in Charlton Crescent where Lady Anne Daventry was killed."

"Ah!" said the inspector quietly. "But I did not say anything about the house in Charlton Crescent or Lady Anne Daventry's death, I think. David Branksome has been arrested for stealing Lady Anne's pearls, not for being concerned in her death."

"He did not!" Margaret Balmaine's voice was as clear as ever.

"How do you know he did not?" The inspector's tone was as determined as hers.

Dorothy and Cardyn looked on much as the seconds in a duel might.

"I know he is innocent—that he did not steal the pearls. Because"—the girl paused and gulped something down in her throat—"I stole them myself!"

"You stole them, Miss Balmaine?" The tone was expressive of nothing but well simulated surprise.

"Yes. I did steal them," Margaret Balmaine reiterated. She stood as she had stood throughout the interview, her head held up defiantly, her clenched hand hanging by her side, the other steadying her against the table behind. "I stole the pearls, I wore your properties"—pointing contemptuously to the wig and bonnet—"I impersonated Lady Anne and got the money from Spagnum's. Now, what are you going to do, Inspector Furnival?"

"Why did you do it?" the inspector questioned, his quiet tone in strong contrast with the fire of hers.

She threw out her hands.

"Can't you see, man? I wanted the money. I have always wanted money, more than I ever had all my life. Here was a chance to get it, to help myself, and I took it. Now, I ask you again, what are you going to do with me? Arrest me, do what you like, only let David Branksome go free."

"I see." The inspector looked at her consideringly. "But this does not account for the bonnet and wig being found in Mr. David Branksome's lodgings or for the footsteps in the flower border. How do you explain these things, Miss Balmaine?"

"Oh, I don't know," she said, her white fingers clutching one another in an agony. "I do not believe in your footmarks at all. I *know* David Branksome was far away from Charlton Crescent when Lady Anne was murdered. As for the wig and bonnet, he found out what I had done and took them away so that no one would suspect me. Why he kept them I don't know. Now—now you must let him out."

The inspector shook his head.

"I have no power to do that. And—I do not know—I doubt whether any jury would believe your story. They would say, I am afraid, that you had invented it to save your lover—"

"How dare you!" the girl interrupted passionately. "It—it had nothing to do with David. I did it on my own. The pearls were of no use to Lady Anne. She never wore them. Very often she told us that she would never wear any jewellery again. She seldom even looked at them. They were shut up in that secret hiding-place in the escritoire—no use to anyone. While to me they meant just—salvation. I took them. I got myself up to look like Lady Anne—I had always been good at theatricals—and was most successful in deceiving Spagnum's."

"How did you manage to get to the escritoire? And without leaving any marks?" the inspector questioned.

"Oh, well!" she hesitated and bit her lip. "After all, most things are possible with skeleton keys."

"A skeleton key would not open or show the secret of the springs," the inspector said dryly. "You will have to think of something else, Miss Balmaine."

"I will not!" she flashed hotly. "I did take them—that is enough for you. I will tell you nothing more. I did take the pearls. How I got them is my own business."

"Yours and Mr. Branksome's," the inspector suggested.

With a glance of supreme contempt Margaret Balmaine turned her back upon him and addressed herself to the other two.

"You do see, don't you, that I did take the pearls? I must say so now that David is arrested. It—it was a sudden temptation. I wanted to have some money while I was young enough to enjoy things. Lady Anne was old. But I wish now that I had not taken her pearls. I would never have touched her to hurt her. Nor would David. You do believe me, do you not?"

"*Qui s'excuse, s'accuse,*" the inspector murmured softly.

Dorothy cast a reproachful glance at him as she laid her arm caressingly round the other girl's back.

"Certainly I believe you, Margaret. I am sure you would not have hurt Lady Anne and I know what temptation is. I—I might have yielded to this myself, if my need had been as great as yours."

"One question," interposed the inspector. "The price of the pearls was paid to you by Spagnum's under the belief that you were Lady Anne Daventry. So much we have discovered, so much you have acknowledged. Now, will you tell us how it was that Miss Fyvert paid the dressmaker's bill with one of the notes you received?" For the first time Margaret Balmaine's eyes fell before his, and a dull flush of shame made itself visible through her powder. She turned from the detective to Dorothy's pitying eyes.

"I changed it, Dorothy. But I did not mean to do you any harm. I did not think the loss of the pearls would be discovered for ages, perhaps not in Lady Anne's lifetime. And then it would have been thought that she had disposed of them herself. If it had not been for those tiresome girls asking to see them that afternoon that is how it would have been, and there would have been no bother at all."

"Poor Aunt Anne!" said Dorothy softly. "I wish she had not found out. It troubled her last moments. But she knows all about it now, Margaret. And—I think we may be sure—she understands."

"Oh, I don't know—we don't know anything." With a quick sob Margaret Balmaine tore herself from the other's embrace.

With his heart in his eyes Bruce Cardyn watched the girl he loved, the pity in her eyes deepening, only the trembling of her lips, her varying colour showing how deeply she was moved. Once he turned towards her impetuously as though to protect her, stand by her. But in a second he checked the impulse and waited.

The inspector was glancing from one to the other sharply. Not one change in their expression escaped him. But his eyes rested last and longest on Margaret Balmaine.

"If there were to be any bother, though," he went on suavely, "you preferred Miss Fyvert to face it sooner than do so yourself. That we all understand, Miss Balmaine. Now it is my painful duty to arrest you for the theft of Lady Anne Daventry's pearls. A taxi is waiting with a couple of officers. But if you will walk quietly downstairs and through the hall with me no one will know anything about it and there need be no unpleasantness."

"Arrested!" Margaret Balmaine swayed.

Dorothy sprang to her side again.

"This is not right, inspector," she cried passionately. "You are exceeding your orders. You—I believe the pearls are mine now, and will not have anyone prosecuted for taking them. You cannot, you dare not take Miss Balmaine away. I will send for her cousin, Mr. John Daventry—you will see that he—"

"Mr. John Daventry is on his way here," said the inspector, glancing at his watch. "I phoned him as soon as I saw the way things were going, and got an answer. He is coming up in his car. As for the pearls, we received instructions from Lady Anne Daventry herself—those instructions were confirmed by her only acting executor, the Rev. and Hon. Augustus Fyvert. I am afraid that even your subsequent inheritance gives you no power to alter them, Miss Fyvert."

"You are taking an unfair advantage," Dorothy said hotly. "We ought to have had some one here to take our part—to—"

"Miss Fyvert," the inspector said gravely, "you must not blame me for what I am doing. I have no choice in the matter, and very soon you will understand that."

"I shall not," Dorothy said stoutly. "I shall always blame you—I will never forgive you if you arrest Margaret. If she goes with you I will come too. I shall tell the magistrate—"

"No," said the inspector firmly. "No one must come with me but my prisoner."

"No," said Margaret Balmaine suddenly. "You cannot come with me, Dorothy. You must not link your young life with my miserable lot. Soon you will learn the worst there is to know about me, and, when you do, will you forgive and pity your poor unhappy Margaret?" She stooped and catching the other girl's hand pressed her lips to it lingeringly. Then she glanced at the inspector. "I am ready," she said simply. "I will come—only be as quick as you can."

Cardyn stepped to the door quickly.

"If I can help you, will you let me for the sake of one who was very dear to us both?" he said to her quietly.

She paused and the inspector waited behind, Dorothy watching them in puzzled amazement.

"You know?" she said simply. "I—I sometimes thought you did."

"Naturally!" he assented. "Because Maisie—"

A sudden light broke over her face.

"Of course! I have been blind all this time. Now I see. You are Maisie's brother!"

He bent his head. "And for her sake, because she loved you and I know how hard life is for women, let me do anything I can for you."

"Help David if you can," she whispered. "Nobody can help me. Only—just believe me—living, I would never have robbed Maisie."

"I am sure you would not," he assented. He held her hand for a moment in his firm clasp, then, dropping it, stood back.

"Good-bye," she whispered. Tell Dorothy—"

She went out, her small golden head held high. The inspector followed closely. Glancing round, Cardyn saw that two men stood further down the passage, that two others were waiting near. They were all in plain clothes, but Cardyn's quick eyes recognized them at once as Inspector Furnival's subordinates. He felt a passing touch of wonder that the inspector's preparations had been so extensive and so thorough. The arrest of one girl like Margaret Balmaine scarcely seemed to call for such strong measures.

But just then he had not time to think of anyone but Dorothy. He went back to her. She was standing as he had left her, near the table opposite the door. He thought she looked terribly ill, worse even than she had in those dreadful days when Maureen was missing. But to his unutterable joy she turned to him now in her trouble. She stretched out her hands to him.

"Tell me how we can help her!"

"The first thing to do is to engage a lawyer for her defence," Bruce answered slowly. "Then, if, as the inheritrix and actual owner of the pearls you plead for her at the trial, her sentence may be lightened. I am afraid it is useless to think of her getting off altogether."

Dorothy interrupted him with a cry of protest.

"It must not—it cannot go to trial. It must be stopped. John's cousin—the old Squire's granddaughter. I think I must be going out of my mind. And—and I was forgetting. You are Balmaine Cardyn—she is your sister and you are letting her go to prison without saying a word to help her! Oh, it is monstrous! monstrous!"

"I should say monstrous too," Cardyn agreed taking the girl's cold hand in his and noting the relief in her eyes as she heard his words. "But—"

"There are no buts," she interrupted him passionately. "I tell you it is monstrous! That you, her brother, should not do anything—lose anything to get her off."

"Yes." Cardyn felt the fingers he still held firmly move, try to detach themselves from his, but he would not release them. Instead he pressed them until his clasp became almost painful.

"Dorothy! I wish it had fallen to anyone but myself to tell you—to break to you—" He stopped short to find words in which to tell her what he knew she had never imagined.

Some of his nervousness communicated itself to Dorothy. She looked at him with eyes in which there lurked an unutterable dread.

"Bruce," she said, using his Christian name for the first time, "don't tell me that you—that anybody thinks—that Aunt Anne—"

"No, no!" he said reassuringly. "I do not think—as far as I know—there is no reason to connect her with Lady Anne's death at all."

"Then what do you mean?" questioned Dorothy. "I—please let me know the worst at once. I don't think I can bear much more," her voice trembling.

"The girl whom you have known as Margaret Balmaine has no claim to the name at all," Bruce Cardyn said steadily. "She is not my sister, she is not old Squire Daventry's granddaughter, but an impostor who successfully deceived poor Lady Anne. An actress known as Daisy Melville."

CHAPTER XXV

DOROTHY TORE her hands from Cardyn's.

"It is not true! She is Margaret Balmaine. Do you think she could have lived with us all this time and none of us have found out?"

"I think it is quite possible," Bruce said steadily. "The facts prove that it is so. The real Margaret Balmaine—Dorothy, you must remember, naturally I knew that this girl was an impostor as soon as I heard Lady Anne mention her name."

"But where is your sister? Why is she not here?"

"My sister—the real Margaret Balmaine—is dead." Bruce paused a moment. "She was on the stage for a short time and this girl who took her name and stole her papers was a great friend of hers. She acted as Daisy Melville."

His words, the certainty of his tone, carried conviction home to Dorothy.

"Then, why," she demanded, "didn't you say so at once? Do you think it was honest to let her remain in Lady Anne Daventry's house, knowing that she was an impostor?"

"Perhaps it was not," Cardyn conceded slowly. "But I was in a difficult position. The impostor was firmly established there; I could offer no proof that she was not what she seemed except my bare word. And you must remember that was there in my professional capacity at Lady Anne Daventry's request, to endeavour to safeguard her life and to discover the secret murderer. I may say at once that when I realized that Miss Balmaine was an impostor I at once formed the opinion that she might be the guilty person, an opinion that was strengthened by the discovery that she was carrying on an intrigue with David Branksome, my predecessor."

Dorothy shivered a little, recalling her own early instinctive shrinking from Margaret Balmaine, a shrinking repugnance that she had almost forgotten of late.

"Yes, yes, I see," she murmured. "But you said—it was not she who—that you did not think that it was she who—who stabbed Aunt Anne."

"I said I was not aware that anything had been discovered to connect her with the crime," Cardyn corrected.

"As I am," Dorothy said bitterly. "Mr. Cardyn, tell me truly, you don't really believe this preposterous story of Inspector Furnival's that one of us—of those five people in the room really murdered Aunt Anne?"

Bruce Cardyn's eyes looked away from her and wandered round the room, rested on the table against which Margaret Balmaine had so lately stood.

"I do not know," he said slowly. "I never have known. I hope not."

"Oh, it is dreadful—dreadful!" Dorothy said passionately. "Nobody is ever sure of anything and one doubts everybody—even oneself. There are times when I wake up in the night and ask myself whether this horror can possibly be true. There are times again when I ask myself over and over again who could have killed Aunt Anne, and I think and think and think until

I doubt every one—even myself. You know Inspector Furnival thinks I did it because I wanted money." Her voice broke.

"You poor child!" Cardyn caught her hands in his. "He does not think—no sane person could possibly think—that you knew anything—that you could possibly be even remotely concerned with anything so terrible. It is just—can't you see that it is only because the inspector is bound to make inquiries about every one of us—that you are brought into the question at all. Otherwise nobody would ever have dreamed of—"

"Oh, yes! Indeed he would—the inspector would," Dorothy said positively. "He would have found that letter of mine all the same and he would have said I had killed her to inherit the jewels. I can't think why he cannot realize—cannot believe that it was—it must have been—an outsider. Don't you think it was that Cat Burglar?" There was some new quality in her tone as she glanced anxiously at Cardyn.

He avoided her glance. "I do not see how the Cat Burglar could have got to the window."

"But you know he did! Don't you think he was guilty?" persisted Dorothy.

Thus driven, Cardyn had to speak out plainly.

"No, I do not. I never have thought it was the Cat Burglar."

Meeting his eyes Dorothy shivered from head to foot. Was some new horror coming upon her? She tore her hands from his clasp and crossing over to the window laid her aching head against the cool wood of the frame.

"I wish I had died with Aunt Anne," she said bitterly.

Cardyn followed her after a minute's pause.

"Dear, you have been very brave so far through this sad time. You must be brave a little longer for the sake of those who love you."

His tone, his words brought a little measure of comfort to Dorothy. Despise his profession as she might, there were times when she could not forget that he was the hero who had saved her from the fire, whose memory she had secretly cherished until Inspector Furnival's words had rudely awakened her from her dream.

She gave a little sob. "You say a little longer, but it goes on day after day, week after week, month after month—why shouldn't it be for year after year? We can none of us do anything, we can none of us think of anything else."

"I wish I could help you—" Cardyn was beginning when the door opened again and Mr. Fyvert looked in. His broad, mild face looked troubled.

"Dorothy, my child, will you go to your aunt? She seems very unwell to-night, and—er—don't say anything to her about this new trouble regarding Margaret. I have told her she has been called out to see some friends. That is quite enough until we know more."

"Yes, Uncle Augustus." Dorothy hesitated a moment, glanced from her uncle to Cardyn, opened her lips as if to speak, then, changing her mind, went quickly out of the room.

The rector stood aside, then he closed the door carefully and came across to Bruce, walking with a silent cat-like tread, curious in so large a person.

"The inspector writes to me that the mystery surrounding my poor sister's death is to be solved to-night. He tells me to come round to her house in Charlton Crescent and to bring you with me. 'At once,' he says in his note; at least"—referring to a paper he produced—"he says 'as soon as you get this.' And this was brought to me a minute or two ago by a man in plain clothes whom I conceived to be a detective."

"Then we had better start at once," Cardyn said quietly.

It was noticeable that he did not ask to see the inspector's note, neither did Mr. Fyvert offer to show it to him.

Mr. Fyvert indeed preserved a silence most unusual for him. He did not speak again until they were getting into their taxi. Then he said, his pompous tones unusually subdued:

"I—er—conclude that when Inspector Furnival speaks of—er—that terrible mystery being solved, he has discovered the murderer?"

"It seems probable," Bruce assented.

"I presume that it has turned out to be the Cat Burglar after all," Mr. Fyvert went on. "Or some member of the criminal classes who had concealed himself in the house for the purpose of robbery and—er—rushed in when you were all looking out of the window. I must say I incline to the latter theory myself."

He turned inquiringly to Bruce, who bent his head, with a murmured assent, looking the while supremely uncomfortable.

Mr. Fyvert glanced at him curiously, but he did not speak again as the taxi glided swiftly up to the house in Charlton Crescent. As they entered the Crescent Cardyn saw that there were men in plain clothes at both ends and also near Lady Anne Daventry's door. Was an arrest to be effected here and now he asked himself, and even his dark face paled as he pictured the scene that might be coming.

Mr. Fyvert, of course, noticed nothing, but as they went up the steps and the door was opened for them by a strange man he looked round uneasily. The inspector met them in the hall.

"I am glad you could come, Mr. Fyvert. It is best that one of the family should—understand."

"Quite so! Though I can't say that I do understand at all at present," the rector said plaintively. "What, for instance, has become of that unhappy girl who called herself Margaret Balmaine?"

"She and her lover, or her husband, as we have good reason to think he is—David Branksome—will be brought before the magistrates in the morning charged with stealing the late Lady Anne's pearls," the inspector said gruffly. "Come this way, please, Mr. Fyvert, and you, Mr. Cardyn."

He opened the library door and ushered them in, and with a murmured apology stepped back into the hall.

"Well, really, I cannot understand—" Mr. Fyvert was beginning helplessly. "I cannot understand—"

Almost as he spoke another taxi drove up and in a very few minutes Inspector Furnival reappeared.

"This way, please, Mr. Soames," he said in his most genial tones as he ushered three men into the room.

Two of them were tall and upstanding and looked as if they would have been more at home in uniform—the one between them Bruce stared at and then rubbed his eyes and stared again. But for the inspector's words he would not have recognized the once consequential, imposing-looking butler of the late Lady Anne Daventry in this bent, prematurely-aged man. The Soames whom Cardyn had seen a hundred times in this very room had always walked in a slow, dignified fashion, shoulders well drawn up and in, figure a little protruding beneath his waistcoat. This Soames tottering in between the two police officers seemed to have shrunk visibly, his cheeks had fallen in, his eyes, turning miserably from side to side, refused to meet any of those amazed ones fixed upon him.

He slunk past Mr. Fyvert, who stepped forward as if to intercept him, and shrank like a dumb animal into the darkest part of the room.

The rector of North Coton turned his astonished eyes upon Inspector Furnival.

"What does this mean, inspector? My poor sister trusted Soames implicitly."

"Ah! Many of us do trust people implicitly, and many of us find ourselves let down pretty badly," the inspector remarked enigmatically. "But very soon we shall know more, Mr. Fyvert. We are expecting one more arrival and then we will set to work."

"One more arrival!" echoed Mr. Fyvert. "Whom do you mean?"

The inspector held up his hand. The hoot of a private car was heard as it turned into the Crescent. Another moment and it had stopped before the door of the house they were in. In the silence induced by the inspector's upheld hand, they heard some one spring out of the car and run up the steps. The bell and knocker were sounded together and a moment later the door was thrown open and a tall man stood on the threshold.

"Ah, Mr. John Daventry, you are just to time," said the inspector easily.

CHAPTER XXVI

"ALWAYS PUNCTUAL," Daventry assented. "Learnt that in the trenches. Ah, Mr. Fyvert"—taking off his motoring gloves and throwing them on the table—"come to be in at the death like me? Come, inspector, what did that urgent wire of yours mean? And what in Heaven's name are you doing with all that bally rubbish?" He pointed to the white mask with its mass of flimsy drapery spreading out upon the table.

The inspector held the mask up gingerly on his forefinger.

"The white face that looked through the window the evening a certain deed of darkness was done, Mr. Daventry."

"What! the Cat Burglar?" John Daventry burst into one of his laughs, causing the rector of North Coton to look at him reprovingly. "Was he masked? You know I always told you, inspector—"

"There was no Cat Burglar," the inspector said gravely. "There was no one at the window at all. There was nothing but a silly trick played by a naughty child and a girl who ought to have known better. This 'bally rubbish,' Mr. Daventry, was lowered from the window of the room above and by attracting everybody in the room to the window gave the murderer time to accomplish his design."

"Maureen and Alice! By Jove!" And Daventry slapped his thigh with another guffaw. "I never gave them credit for so much iniquity. And who was the murderer who rushed in and accomplished his fell design, inspector? That is the most interesting point. Have you got him?"

"I think so!" said the inspector quietly. He stood aside and revealed the shivering Soames, whom he had been purposely concealing from Daventry's view.

A curious change visible only to the closest observer passed over John Daventry's face. For a moment he seemed to stiffen, like a man who had received a blow in the face.

"What—old Soames! Bless my life, inspector, what nonsense are you up to?" Then he turned aside and blew his nose vigorously. "Upon my soul, inspector, how you could—"

"Mr. John, Mr. John!" The words came from Soames, though the hoarse thickened voice was in odd contrast with the butler's erstwhile self-sufficient tones.

They all stared at him, John Daventry among them. The man's mottled face was quivering, his bloodshot eyes were watering, the loose lips were working, twitching, the shoulders were hunching themselves up, the whole man seemed on the verge of collapse.

"Mr. John—I couldn't help it—I never meant it. I was forced—I was tricked—" The uneven voice broke off in a gurgle, the ghastly face was hidden by a pair of trembling hands.

A great silence fell upon them all in the room. Even Inspector Furnival and Bruce Cardyn, hardened criminal hunters though they were, felt their breathing quicken.

A loud guffaw from John Daventry broke across the stillness with the force of an electric shock.

"So the game's up, is it, old Soames? I guessed it would be when the inspector guessed the Cat Burglar business. Don't worry, old chap. You have done your best! Inspector, I congratulate you!"

Something jingled in the inspector's hands, the next moment it was round John Daventry's wrist and the room seemed instantly full of men in plain clothes surrounding them both.

"John William Daventry"—the inspector's stern voice dominated them all—"I arrest you for the wilful murder of Anne Georgina Dorothea Daventry in this house on the evening of January. And it is my duty to warn you that anything you say will be taken down in writing and may be used in evidence against you."

"You bet it will!" Again that loud laugh of Daventry's rang through the room. "Damn it all man, I can see when the game is up. And I don't know that I care much. It seemed a wicked shame that that old woman should go on living—a life that was no good to herself or anyone else. Stingy old beggar too. Made as much fuss about lending a chap a few pounds as though she hadn't got any amount of shekels tucked away in the bank. Seemed as if she was going to live for ever, and that beastly rheumatism doesn't kill. I might have been too old to enjoy the stuff when it did come. So I took the matter in my own hands. But it hasn't done me much good and I don't know that I'm sorry it has ended as it has. Sometimes in the night I have seen the old thing's eyes looking up at me as they did when I stuck the dagger in. So that is the end, inspector. And don't touch old Soames. He knew nothing about it until it was all over when he saw me taking my hand from the dagger. But you won't have your sensational trial, inspector. I have laid my plans too well for that! Good-bye, everybody. It is going over the top of the trench a bit before my time, that is all." With the last words he staggered against the wall.

"Poison—that handkerchief! And I never thought of it?" the inspector explained as he and another man caught up the prisoner.

"Good old blow, wasn't it?" Daventry managed to get the words out as the men surrounded him. "You will find the half of a tablet there that would kill a dozen men, inspector."

The words were haltingly spoken. The hue of death was spreading over the handsome features. The policemen laid him back on the couch; the eyes were glazing over, the breath was failing.

Soames stumbled forward and fell beside him.

"Mr. John! Mr. John—you'd never have done it in your right mind. It was the gas and the shells in that accursed war! Up there they'll know it all—and understand."

And that was the requiem of John Daventry.

"Oh, a terrible affair, terrible!" the rector of North Coton said. "And, inspector, I hear that the poor boy's grandmother on the maternal side had periodical attacks of insanity. I take it that the poor fellow must have inherited the taint."

"Perhaps." The inspector's tone was doubtful.

All that was mortal of John Daventry had been laid to rest in the churchyard at Daventry nearly a month ago. And Mr. Fyvert and the inspector were just "tidying up," as the inspector phrased it, in the library at Charlton Crescent.

"There was that terrible shell shock too that he got in the trenches," the rector pursued. "He and a party of his men were buried by the explosion of a shell close at hand and had to be dug out. Then he was badly gassed. Such experiences must leave their mark, you know, inspector. John Daventry could not be looked upon as accountable for his actions."

The inspector's face was very grave. He made no motion of assent. Presently Mr. Fyvert went on: "How was it that you suspected him, inspector? For I gather that you did suspect him."

"It was fairly obvious, was it not?" the inspector said with a sarcasm that was lost upon the rector. "Well, I may say that I did not think of him at first. My suspicions were divided between that unhappy girl, Branksome's wife—whom very early in the proceedings I discovered to be an impostor—and Soames. It was very soon obvious that the butler was either guilty himself or screening some one. The footprints on the border to which he drew my attention were a clumsy device; he has since confessed that he used an old pair of Branksome's shoes to make them, fastening them firmly to a pole and leaning from the window to stamp them on the soft earth beneath."

The rector's mild eyes opened wide. "What an extraordinary device! It would never have occurred to me."

"I am sure it would not," the inspector agreed heartily, a faint twinkle in his eye. "Then I found out that Soames had been for some time in a chemist's shop in his youth. That would have given him the knowledge necessary for the making up of the hyoscine pill—the poison in the milk. Pirnie suspected him too. It seems she thought that while he was philandering with her he had taken the opportunity to poison the milk. However, she knows the truth now and they have made it up. So that is all right. And I discovered that both John Daventry and Lady Anne's eldest son, Christopher had had a turn that way and had messed about with drugs a good deal as boys under Soames's tuition. That I think first turned my suspicions definitely to John Daventry. He knew about the attempted secret poisoning of Lady Anne and he did not tell us of Soames's knowledge."

"I cannot think that poor John knew anything of the attempted poisoning," remarked Mr. Fyvert fatuously.

The inspector contented himself with raising his eyebrows.

"Then again he had obviously fallen in love with the pretended Miss Balmaine," he pursued. "That provided an additional motive. Though no doubt his financial difficulties were the principal. My very definite suspicion became a certainty when I taxed Soames with his share in the matter."

"Yes! Yes! I see!" The rector blew his nose vigorously. "Poor John—poor John! Well think it may be said that gassed and shellshocked as he had been he gave his life for his country as truly as any of those who fell on the field of battle. I am sure my poor sister will agree with me with the clearer vision of Eternity."

The inspector coughed dubiously. "I hope so."

"And that unhappy girl—David Branksome's wife?" questioned Mr. Fyvert after a pause.

"David Branksome himself is a professional crook," Inspector Furnival answered. "His wife is an actress who successfully made up to impersonate Lady Anne. She dressed at her husband's lodgings where I found most of the garments. But the gown she made herself at Charlton Crescent and kept there. She it was who stole the diary with the help of her husband's instruments, and he managed to get the pearls while he was secretary to Lady Anne. The pearls, of course, were their principal objective; but there can be no doubt that they hoped to obtain other jewellery, and it was their desire to possess themselves of the diamonds that led to their undoing, since they might have got off safely with the pearls."

"Oh, dear! Oh, dear! It is all very sad and terrible," sighed the rector. "That child Maureen, too, has probably injured herself for life by that foolish trick with the mask. Oh, I am very much afraid so." As the inspector made a gesture of dissent. "They are going to take her abroad very soon—the sister and Mr. Cardyn, for I dare say you will be surprised to hear that they—Miss Fyvert and Bruce Cardyn—are going to be married very quietly and quite soon."

The inspector raised his eyebrows. "Indeed! I had not heard."

"No? It may seem soon after all—the—the trouble. But it is quite a long standing attachment, they tell me, and they are anxious to get away from all this talk of 'the five' and the tragedy altogether. Still, most people are surprised like you, inspector. For myself—I suppose my profession renders me unusually observant—I was expecting the announcement, from various little signs that have noticed."

The inspector made no rejoinder, but later on when the rector had gone, he said to himself, rubbing his nose reflectively, "Wonder *what* he noticed. Profession made him observant, has it? About as observant as Balaam, I should think, when the ass had to speak to make him stop. And the ass would have had to shout pretty loud to stop the rector of North Coton."

THE END

Made in the USA
Coppell, TX
26 January 2022

72388986R00108